Charline Norton

Outskirts Press, Inc.
Denver, Colorado

This is a work of fiction. The events and characters described herein are imaginary and are not intended to refer to specific places or living persons. The opinions expressed in this manuscript are solely the opinions of the author and do not represent the opinions or thoughts of the publisher. The author has represented and warranted full ownership and/or legal right to publish all the materials in this book.

Surviving 5th Grade

v4.0

Outskirts Press, Inc.
http://www.outskirtspress.com

ISBN: 978-1-4327-6243-8

Library of Congress Control Number: 2010939593

PRINTED IN THE UNITED STATES OF AMERICA

Acknowledgment:

Special thanks go to my family, my colleagues and friends, my students, and my husband who inspired and encouraged me to follow my dream.

Dedication:

For all the Grandkids

Meghan, Julie, Jackson,
Allison, Tori, Charlie,
Josh, Ben, Rachel,
Addison, and my Angel, Roxanne

Chapter One
School Daze—Who Cares?

"Too bad we can't just freeze today forever," said Tank, tossing his stuff-bag next to a river rock.

"Yeah. Like forever AND ever," said Spencer.

Best friends, Tank, Spencer, Zach, and Alex spread beach towels in the shade of a tree close to the withering river. August heat had reduced the once rushing water to random swimming holes and mossy green puddles. Shadow Falls had become a mere trickle. Even so, the boys were intent on devouring every last bit of summer vacation, freedom, and do-nothing days. They opened paper bag lunches, offered trades, and began to eat.

Tank sat cross-legged munching his squashed Twinkie and stared through the canopy of leaves into the deep blue of a late summer sky. He leaned against the tree and sucked in a long breath of warm air.

"Don't this beat all? I mean, ain't this the life? No school, no homework, no stupid reports." Tank locked his fingers behind his head and kept talking.

"Soon as school starts, my life's out the window. It'll be a miracle if I even survive 5th grade. I *got* to get me some kinda life."

"Some kinda life? What's that s'posed to mean?" asked Spencer.

"Yeah. What're you talkin' about, Tank?" spluttered Alex through a mouthful of potato chips. "We all got to do 5th grade. Even if it takes a bunch of miracles."

The boys stared at Tank. School buddies since Kindergarten, they were used to putting up with his shenanigans and unpredictable behavior, but this was different. Not the usual Tank-talk.

"Forget it. It's stupid." Tank backed off; embarrassed the words had spilled out of his mouth.

"Come on, Tank, give," said Zach. "You in trouble or somethin'?"

"Ain't no secrets with us guys," said Alex. "We took a spit oath on stuff like that. So no secrets."

Tank picked up a stone and rolled it around in his hand. He tossed the stone toward the river. "Dang. Spit-promise to drop it if I tell?"

"Sure," said Spencer. He looked at the other boys. They spit in their hands and crossed their hearts.

"So what's eatin' you?"

"It's you guys. You always got it made. Yer smart, yer good at sports and ya got nice families—'cept for your pesty little sister, Spence. But me? What do I got? A big fat zero. Nothin'. Plain ol' nothin'."

"Heck if I know what you're talkin' about," said Zach, stuffing another cookie in his mouth.

"You got a cool mom, Tank." Alex attempted encouragement. "You play soccer good. Look at the Zach-man. His dad's off to some place doin' stuff in the army. He don't have a whole big family. Least ways not now."

"I *know* that," said Tank. "But, he's *got* a dad. I don't. Besides, everybody thinks I'm stupid. I got to have special classes and stuff." He crooked his fingers around the word special. "There. I'm a stupid fat kid with this dumb red hair, no dad, and Mom never lets me stay over at anybody's house. Shoot. I ain't even got a fish."

"You sick or somethin'?" Zach never figured Tank to be anything but upbeat and ready to take on the world.

"Don't ya get it? Next week. It's school, and everythin' starts all over," said Tank. "Same ol' stuff. School, and principal, and homework, and trouble, or somethin' else. The whole thing stinks. Nothin' ever changes for me. How much ya wanna bet I even get that crotchety old 'Wonderbuns Gunderson'. She'll prob'ly send me to the office right off."

"Sounds about right when you put it *that* way," said Spencer.

"Maybe you could try harder." Alex sat up, momentarily distracted from his sand drawing. He was never without something to sketch on, even if it was only the dirt around him.

"That's bull-o-nee!" said Tank. "Ya *know* I don't do stuff on purpose. Shoot, I just get blamed for everythin'." Tank frowned and picked at the white filling in his second Twinkie. "Just once I wish things could go my way. Even those goofy girls hate me. Especially Ellie. She's so stuck up an' mean. Treats me like I got bat boogers, or rabies." He licked at the gooey marshmallow filling. "Ah, heck. Who cares anyway?"

"I do," said Spencer. "Right guys?" Spencer always had Tank's back.

"Maybe you just gotta think different," said Zach. He stood up and brushed cookie crumbs off his chest. As far as Zach was concerned, school was just an inconvenience. His whole ambition in life was to become a professional athlete. "Get your attitude adjusted or somethin', Tank. Be extra nice."

"Yeah, right. Anyways, we ain't fixin' anything today, so drop it. One thing's for sure though."

"What?" asked Alex. He picked up another stick to finish his design.

"We're finally off restriction for messin' up Ellie's sleepover last week. Geez, I hate bein' grounded. The girls are prob'ly thinkin' up somethin' to get even with us, and we're just wastin' our brains talkin' about it."

"Got that right," said Zach.

"So let's go swimmin'. Prob'ly be our last chance before DOOMSDAY," said Tank.

"What're we waitin' for?" yelled Spencer. He wadded up his empty lunch bag and threw it at Alex who was still doodling in the sand.

"Shoot, Spence! You messed up my design."

"Soorrr-eeee," said Spencer. "Didn't know it was anything special." Spencer had grown so used to Alex's constant obsession with drawing and doodling that he thought nothing of interrupting his friend. "Last one in is a rotten egg!" he yelled.

"Oh, yeah?" With renewed ambition, Tank started for the water first. "Can't beat me!" he shouted.

The foursome picked their way over the jumble of river rocks to the swimming hole and jumped in. "Yaaa . . . hooo!" yelled Tank. "Now *this* really *is* more like it!" He tossed a dead crawdad at Alex and hit him on the nose.

"Watch it, Tank! I'll get you for that!" Alex hurled a big clump of water moss at Tank. Tank ducked the flying algae and took off after Alex with a fistful of mud.

The boys didn't know they were being watched. Long-time

classmates, Mia, Becca, and Ellie went looking for the boys after learning they had gone to the river to celebrate getting off restriction. Finding them was easy. The yelling and splashing coming from a favorite swimming hole was a dead give away. From the seclusion of a large boulder, they spied on their tormentors. They were looking for something, anything to get even.

Chapter 2
Mia's Getting-Even Idea

"Got an idea," said Mia. "More of a plan actually. Told you I'd think of somethin' to get even with those guys."

Mia, Becca, and Ellie attended school with Tank and company from day one. And every year, the competitive rivalry between them continued to grow. The neighborhood bunch couldn't resist playing silly pranks and annoying tricks on each other, most of which were specifically detailed in Ellie's diary. After the boys ruined Ellie's last summer sleep-over, the girls *had* to think up some kind of pay-back to get even with them.

Becca glared at Mia over her glasses. "Too many ideas, Mia. Your ideas usually get you in trouble. Get us in trouble."

"Not always. I know this'll work," said Mia. "Those guys deserve a get-back for ruining your sleepover, Ellie. Grab your diary. You'll want to get this down for sure."

"Before I write *anything*, Mia, let's hear this *wild* idea of yours," said Ellie. "We don't need trouble, especially when school's about to start."

"Well, check it out," said Mia. "The guys left all their stuff by the tree. We can sneak over, grab their junk and hide it. They won't know it was us. They're too busy showin' off for each other."

"Oh, sure, Mia. Wanna bet? They'll figure it out all right. Then *we'll* be in trouble for messing with their stupid stuff." Becca delivered a no nonsense response. Mia just shrugged her shoulders.

"Well, I for one don't want to touch their slimy stuff. Those guys have cooties, and their shoes probably stink," said Ellie.

"What do you mean *probably*? You *know* they're gross." Becca looked over her glasses and shoved them to the bridge of her nose. "Every Friday my stupid brother dumps his stinky shoes and sweaty gym clothes right on top of *my* laundry basket. He thinks it's funny."

"That's disgusting," said Ellie. "Glad I don't have any brothers, or sisters for that matter. Just me, myself, and I. Perfect."

"Okay, Miss Perfect," said Mia. "We got it." *At least my brother's at college.*

"Back to my plan. All we have to do is take their towels by the corners with all their junk and toss everything into the trash can by the bike trail. We won't have to touch anything that way. But if we're gonna do it, we got to do it now. They won't stay in the water forever. Come on. Let's get 'em back."

"Wait," said Ellie. "Look at those fools. They're acting like complete idiots. I will absolutely barf if we have to be in the same class with those dorks again this year. Especially that loud-mouth, Twinkie-stuffing, trouble-maker Tank. He is *so* weird."

"Those guys don't know how to dress either." Ellie rattled on. "Did you see Spencer's trunks? Looks like he's wearing his sister's shorts! Okay, Mia, you win. I have *got* to write this down. This is too hilarious."

"Stop talking, Ellie," said Mia. "You can write it down *after* we dump their stuff. We got to move quick if we're gonna do this."

"Well, someone has to be the talker, or reporter, or whatever," said Ellie. "How else will my *friends and fans* know what's going on?" She giggled. "Anyway, it's fun to read this stuff at my parties."

"Right. But I hope your next party has a better ending. What a disaster." said Becca.

"Okay," said Ellie. "You win. The guys definitely deserve a get-back. Let's do it. Let's hide their stuff." She tucked her diary under her arm and slid her fancy pink pen behind her ear. "Come on you guys."

"Right behind you, Ellie. Hurry!" said Becca.

Chapter 3
The Slumber Party

It was at Ellie's last sleep-over of the summer that the boys managed to spoil everything. She had arranged a party with Becca, Mia, and the Meyer twins, Jan and Joan. Ellie phoned everyone with the same message:

"Dad'll set up the tent in the back yard. Rufus can be our guard dog. He'll probably want to sleep in the tent with us anyway. Can you come? Be here about four. We'll swim and order pizza. I'll even share some secret stuff I've written in my diary!"

Of course, everyone accepted.

Ellie's dad set the tent up between the house and the back fence. Close enough to hear a call for help if needed, and far enough from the house so the girls could talk long into the night without annoying anyone.

Rufus, the big family mutt, ducked in and out of the tent nearly knocking it down several times. "Rufus! Get out!" yelled Ellie. "You're messing everything up. Go away. D A A A A D!"

Rufus took the hint and sulked off to find an old bone he had stashed behind the woodpile. He brought it back and flopped down to gnaw on the grubby remains.

Ellie decorated everything for the last summer sleep-over. "Everyone's going to remember *this* party." She spoke softly to Rufus. "Isn't it just too cool?" He lifted his head and wagged his tail.

By the time the girls had their last swim, finished their pizza, and arranged the tent the way they wanted, it was almost dark. Shouts and squeals turned into giggling and the usual shuffle for space.

Move over! Your elbow's in my face. Don't step on my glasses. Where's my pillow? Have you seen my other sock? My zipper's stuck. You still like Spencer?

Why? He is such a nerd. Who wants to hold the light while I read something from my diary?

"You girls have your flashlights?" called Dad. "I don't want any of you falling into the pool if you need to come in the house tonight."

"We're fine, Dad," Ellie answered.

"Keep the radio down, too. No need for neighbors phoning us in the middle of the night. G'night everybody."

"G'night," called the girls.

"Ouch!"

"Lay down, Rufus."

"Yuk! Dog breath!"

Chapter 4
Big Trouble

"I don't know if this is such a good idea," said Alex. He and Spence stood outside Spencer's house in the early evening darkness, waiting for Tank and Zach.

"Hey, as long as nobody gets hurt, you know our parents won't care," said Spencer. "What can happen besides nothin'? We'll just give the girls a little scare and have a good laugh."

Zach jogged up to the boys at the designated meeting place out of breath.

"You get everything?" asked Spencer.

"Yep," said Zach, bending over to catch his breath. "Tank was s'posed to bring a big ol' bone for Rufus, but guess what? He's grounded again. So I got us a big fat bone and the other stuff, too. Bet we really get the girls good this time."

"I hope Ellie's dad doesn't get too mad," said Alex. "I'll be in big trouble if *my* dad finds out about this."

"So who's gonna tell?" asked Spencer. "Don't worry. Besides, you guys are spendin' the night. With any luck, we'll be in and out of the yard in a flash and back to my house."

"How much you wanna bet the girls'll figure out it was us?" asked Zach. "They aren't stupid."

"Whatever," said Spencer. "We can deal with that later."

Spencer, Alex, and Zach trotted down to Ellie's with the 'goods' in hand. Spencer recited directions while they jogged. Alex had some doubts.

"You're crazy, Spence. You really think we can pull this off?"

"Piece o' cake," said Spencer. "When we get to Ellie's back gate, we got to be real quiet. We'll be able to hear if the girls are making any noise. Rufus'll prob'ly start barking. That's when I whisper-like call him over, and you give him that bone, Alex. Right?"

"Okay."

"Then," Spencer continued, "we sneak into the yard and listen for the girls' blabbing. Zach, you hang onto the container."

"Okay, but how we gonna get these things *inside* the tent?"

"Not a problem," explained Spencer. "I'll go around one side, and Alex'll go on the other—really quiet like. You sneak up by the front, Zach. On the count of a silent three, Alex and me'll lift the flaps and you roll the open jar into the tent. Then we sprint like crazy back to the gate. Got it? We can hide outside the gate and wait for the action."

"Right," said Zach. "Boy, this ought to be good!"

The boys reached Ellie's back gate and looked around for any unexpected interference. "Everybody ready?" whispered Spencer.

"Ready."

"Let's go then." Spencer opened the back gate. It creaked a little. Rufus heard.

Chapter 5
Surprise!

"Rufus! Be quiet!" commanded Ellie. "Lay down!"

"What's he barking at?" asked one of the twins.

"Ouch! Get off, Rufus! Where's he going?" asked Becca.

"Prob'ly chasing the neighbor's cat," said Ellie. "Don't worry, he'll be back. Turn up this song. I love it."

Rufus ran to the back gate, took off with the bone offering, and ignored the boys sneaking into the yard. They crept through the darkness toward the tent. A radio was playing, and the girls were singing along to their favorite song.

"This is going to be easier than I thought," whispered Spencer. "They won't hear us at all. Come on. Get up front, Zach."

Zach's heart was pounding. He stood near the front of the tent and watched Alex and Spencer creep to either side of the tent. They moved like lions stalking prey. Zach unscrewed the lid on the jar and waited for his cue. Spencer counted by raising his fingers: *1 . . . 2 . . . 3 . . .* "*Now!*" he mouthed.

Spencer and Alex lifted the flaps. Zach rolled the open jar into the tent, and the three of them high-tailed it to the back gate. Once on the outside, they looked at each other and listened. It wasn't long before the squealing started. Then they took off for Spencer's house.

"Told ya it would be a piece o' cake," said Spencer. "Almost too easy."

"What's that? Something's on my pillow! Yikes! It's cold—and wet! What's on my head?" The screams got louder and more frantic by the second.

"Turn on your flashlight, Becca!" yelled Ellie. "Rufus where are you? Come here! D A A A A D!"

By now the tent was alive with some thirty hopping frogs and five leaping girls. Rufus dashed into the tent with one mighty leap, hit the supports, and brought the whole thing down.

Dad shot out the back door and raced down the steps. When he got to the tent, he searched for the opening. "What happened? Everyone okay?"

Rufus came boiling out first and gave himself a hefty shake. Then Dad lifted a corner of the tent and helped the panicked, screaming girls.

"What in heaven's name is going on?" yelled Ellie's mother as she ran down the back steps still tying her bathrobe. "Is everyone all right?"

"Looks like we had visitors," said Dad. He stared into the darkness searching for any sign of movement.

"These wet, slimy things started jumping in my hair and on my face," said Mia. "At first I didn't know what it was. Then I shined my flashlight on Becca. It was frogs! *Millions of frogs*—everywhere! I almost got everything under control until Rufus jumped in and the tent caved. I wasn't scared. Not really."

"Yeah, sure," said Ellie. "Like *you* were gonna save us, Mia?"

"My glasses! I can't find them," moaned Becca. "I'm dead without them."

"Well, look at me. My new pajamas are all slimed up with frog gunk. Will this come out, Mom?" whined Ellie. "Eeee-yuk."

The twins just stared at each other not knowing whether to laugh or cry. Ellie's mom moved into the fray. "Let's untangle this mess, girls, and keep an eye out for Becca's glasses. Get everything in the house and we'll sort things there."

Rufus chased the fleeing frogs all over the yard while Dad began quizzing the girls.

"Okay girls. Any ideas on what happened or who might have done this?"

Becca, Mia and Ellie looked at each other. "The guys, of course!" They said it like it was rehearsed.

"Who else could possibly have gotten into the yard without Rufus tearing them to shreds?" said Ellie.

"Yeah, it had to be them," said Mia.

"We'll find out soon enough. Everyone into the house," said Dad. I'll give Spencer's father a call. See if we can get to the bottom of this." At the Johnson house, the phone rang a few times, and Spencer's dad answered.

"Hello?"

"Eric? Jess Covington here. Sorry to bother you, but we've had a little trouble tonight with Ellie's sleep-over and some frogs."

"Frogs?"

"That's right. Frogs. I was wondering . . . um, if Spencer's still up, he may know something about this. Could you ask him?"

"Far as I know he's in his room," said Eric. *"Alex and Zach are spending the night. I think they're watching a movie or playing video games. Hang on. I'll go check."*

Spencer's dad knocked on the bedroom door. When there was no response, he looked in and saw three sleeping bags neatly lined up on the floor, looking very much occupied.

"Hey, Jess? Seems the boys have gone to sleep. Tank's not here. You might give his mom a call. Maybe he knows something. Sorry the girls' party was ruined. I hope everyone's okay."

"They're fine. We'll get it figured out. Thanks, Eric. Talk to you later. Call if you hear anything."

Mr. Covington hung up the phone, dialed Tank's mom, and went through the same routine. Tank was indeed grounded, had been with her all evening, and was made to go to bed early.

"Okay, girls. Here's what we know. Alex and Zach are at Spencer's house. Tank's grounded, and the boys are asleep."

Ellie's dad relayed the news to the group while her mom made hot chocolate and had the girls arrange their sleeping bags in the den.

"I just know it was them," said Ellie. "Had to be. Tank must've heard me talking about my sleep-over at the store yesterday when he was with his Momm-eee." Her voice mimicked a two year old. "He's such a loud-mouth. He prob'ly told the guys about it." *Why can't he ever just shut up and mind his own business?*

"Well, you girls get to sleep," said Mr. Covington. "Tomorrow's another day. We'll get some answers then." He was pretty sure the boys had *something* to do with the evening's fiasco, too.

"Found your glasses, Becca," said Mrs. Covington. "Looks like they're okay."

"Gee, thanks, Mrs. Covington. I'd be lost without 'em."

"Good night again, girls," said Mrs. Covington. "See you in the morning."

Chapter 6
The Morning After

"Thanks for the exciting party, Ellie," said Jan. "I can't remember being at a sleep-over with frogs, dogs, and falling tents. It was really fun! Call us if you find out anything."

Jan and Joan's mom loaded the twins and all their paraphernalia into the car. "'Bye everybody. We're going school shopping. See you next week. Thanks for everything," said Joan. "Mom," said Jan, "you're never going to believe what happened last night!"

Mia and Becca hung around to help Ellie clean up and scour the yard for possible frog-caper clues.

"I just know it was those guys," said Ellie. "And that . . . that stupid Tank *had* to be the big blabber mouth. Search the yard. Maybe we'll find something." *Why does Tank always have to be such a big jerk?*

"Okay," said Mia, "But make it quick. I got to get some school stuff today, too. Mom promised. Have to admit it though."

"What?" asked Ellie.

"That really *was* some party," said Mia. "Now we've got to get even. Never fear. I'll think of something."

Becca gave her glasses a nudge and surveyed the back yard for anything out of the ordinary. "Hey!" she shouted. "Rufus has a piece of paper in his mouth. Get him before he eats it!"

"Rufus! Get over here!" called Ellie. She chased him toward the house. "Head him off, Mia! Grab his collar, Becca!"

"Let go, Rufus!" shouted Ellie. She struggled to get the little paper from his mouth. Rufus finally let go but not before the paper was drenched with dog goobers and slobber.

"Yuk, and double yuk!" exclaimed Ellie as she untangled the slimy paper. "Looky here. This looks like it was one of Alex's drawings. See the little A M in the corner? 'Alex Medina'. He must've dropped it . . . last night? A genuine clue, dontcha think, girls? Let's show dad. I know we're right. You can bet it was the guys who let all those frogs go in the tent."

"Sure looks incriminating," said Dad, not in the least surprised when Ellie presented the wet and crinkled paper to him. "I'll give Spencer's dad a call again since the boys were at his house last night. If Alex is still there, we might be able to get a confession." He reached for the phone, and it rang before he could pick it up.

"Hello? Oh, hello Eric. Is that right? So they admitted it? Wow, that's too bad. Is he all right? Okay then. Thanks for the call. I'll let the girls know."

"Right you are, girls. The boys were the culprits. I guess Tank *did* tell them about the party. While they were running back to Spencer's last night, Alex tripped and took a nose dive onto the pavement. He got pretty skinned up so they couldn't sneak back into the house without getting caught. Spencer's mom got Alex cleaned up and called his parents. Everyone's grounded of course—even Tank. A lot of it was his idea."

"I thought you said they were asleep at Spencer's," said Mia.

"Well, apparently they stuffed their sleeping bags with clothes and pillows to make it look like someone was inside. They figured they'd be back before anyone found out they were gone, but because of Alex's accident, everyone had to confess that they were over here last night."

"I knew it, I knew it, I knew it!" cheered Ellie. "I knew it was them. Serves 'em right. This really *was* some party. Are we good detectives, girls, or what?" *Stupid Tank. Might have known he was at the bottom of this.*

"You're right, Mia," said Ellie. "They deserve everything they got. Now we definitely have to get 'em back."

"Think that's such a good idea?" asked Becca. "Now that the whole *frog* thing is over, and they're in big trouble anyway?"

"And why not?" asked Mia. "Just wait 'til they're off restriction."

It didn't take long.

Chapter 7
Back on Shore, Lost and Found

Wet and chilled after their off-restriction-celebration-swim, the boys shivered their way back to the sycamore tree and dashed for their towels.

"Hey! Where's my towel? I know I left my towel here . . . right . . . here," said Alex, pointing at the ground. "My shoes, shorts, everything. Gone!"

"*All* our stuff's gone," said Zach, turning a tight circle and examining the area.

"Wait a minute. There's something fishy here," said Spencer.

Tank and Spencer looked at each other. "THE GIRLS!" They said it together. "Bet they followed us," said Spencer. "Prob'ly getting us back for crashing Ellie's party."

"Don't bring *that* up again," begged Alex. "It cost me a bunch of days being grounded, and I had to do all my brothers' chores."

"Ya think it could have been Old Man Potter? Pot-zee's always down here in the river bottom collectin' stuff," said Tank. "He's such a weird dude. Crazy maybe, too. Wonder what he does with all that junk he collects? We should call him Old Potter-Pots-'n-Pans."

"Nah, I don't think it was him," said Spencer. "Look at the footprints. They're too small. And they're everywhere."

"Okay. So where's our stuff?" asked Alex. "Check it out. Look where the prints go." Zach examined the footprints on the ground like he was a master detective. "They head this way. No. Over here. Shoot. They're all over the place."

"How we ever gonna find anything?" Alex asked no one in particular.

"Let's split up," said Spencer. "Tank, you go that way." He pointed down river. "Zach, you go up river, and Alex and me'll scout around here. Don't get too far, and if you find something, give a holler. If we don't find anything after a few minutes, we'll know the girls, or Old Man Potter, or somebody just took off with everything."

The boys danced and jigged barefoot over rocks and hot sand. "Shoooooot!" Tank's voice echoed up and down the river letting the world know he had stubbed his toe. *Why'd I get the rockiest part? Thanks Spence.* He rubbed his foot for a few minutes, and then hobbled back toward the meeting place empty handed.

"Come here, you guys! We found our stuff!" yelled Alex.

"Over here in the trash can! Looks like everything's here," said Spencer. He began hauling towels, and shoes, and shirts out of the metal drum. "And look what I found." He held up Ellie's diary and waved it over his head. "Eureka! We've struck gold!"

Chapter 8
The Moment of Truth

There was no doubt as to who had taken their things, but what to do about the girls' trick generated all kinds of creative ideas.

"I think we should tell on the girls," said Tank. "Would serve 'em right. We should get *them* in trouble for trashing our stuff."

"I got a better idea," said Spencer. "Let's *read* the diary first. We might find some good ammunition for future get-backs. Might even be some stuff about us in it."

"Maybe," said Zach, "and if we keep our mouths shut, the girls'll think they got away with tricking us, and Ellie will keep wondering what happened to her stupid diary."

"You're right, Zach." Alex was convinced something could be gained by saying nothing and keeping the diary. "Wonder if there's anything about me in there?"

"Let's find out," said Spencer. "We can read it when we get back to my house. Come on!"

The boys could have set a world speed record at the rate they ran to Spencer's house. The back door flew open and they slid around the corner like a herd of buffalo.

"Hey! Slow down, fellas." Spencer's dad called after the boys as they made a mad dash for Spencer's room. "What's the big hurry?"

"Nothin', Dad. We just want to get into some dry clothes. We'll be back in a few. Need something?"

"No. Just slow it down. By the way, your mother wants to know if the boys can stay for dinner tonight."

"Great!" said Spencer. "I'll ask 'em."

"Let her know ASAP. She's making your favorite. Spaghetti."

"Sure thing, Dad."

Spencer closed the bedroom door and braced it with a chair so his little sister couldn't come in. The four boys huddled around their new found treasure.

"Hurry, Spence! Open the diary," said Tank. "Must be some great stuff in there."

"I am. I am," said Spencer. "Just hold on." Spencer held the diary while the boys crowded around and he shared the contents.

"Well, page one is a big nothin'. Look. Just a bunch of girly stuff. Ellie's writin' about clothes and hair. Page two and three . . . more clothes. Pictures of Mia, Becca, and Ellie painting their nails. Not a whole bunch."

They were so intent on reading Ellie's diary they hardly heard the knock on the door. "Shh. I think I hear something," said Alex.

"Can I come in?" Spencer's little sister, Amy, was at the door.

"Not now, Amy," said Spencer. "I'm busy."

"But I wanna come in." She knocked harder.

"NO, Amy. I said I'm busy. You'll have to wait. Us guys have important school talk right now. Besides we're changin' clothes."

"I'm telling Mamma on you," said Amy. "I am five and one half, and I have school talk, too. I'm going to Kindergarten, you know."

"How 'bout I give you a dime if you go away? And don't go tellin' Mom I won't let you in. You can talk school stuff with us later," said Spencer. "After dinner I'll give you a dime. That's TEN whole pennies. Okay?"

"Amy held up her fingers and counted. "Ten pennies is ten dimes."

"No, Amy. Oh, forget it. I promise you'll get your dime," said Spencer. "And I even crossed my heart."

"I get a dime. I get some pennies." Amy's voice trailed off as she sang her little pennies and dimes song. "And don't tell Mamma." She repeated Spencer's directions.

"Like that's gonna work? Come on, Spence," said Tank. "Amy'll blow our cover for sure. Get back to the book. We're wastin' time."

"Okay, okay. Give me a break." Spencer was frustrated by his sister's interruption. He thumbed ahead a few pages. Suddenly, his own name practically jumped off the page. In another spot, there were the other names: Tank, Alex and Zach.

"Pay dirt," whispered Spencer.

"Let's see! Le'me see!" said Alex. "What's it say?"

"Hold it, guys. Not yet," said Spencer. He closed the diary.

"Geez, Spence," moaned Tank. "What the heck are ya doin'?"

"Sorry guys. First things first. Can you all stick around for dinner? Mom's waiting for an answer. She's makin' spaghetti. Then after dinner we can *really* examine this specimen."

No one had trouble getting permission to stay, but the wait for dinner to be over was agonizing. Amy kept looking suspiciously at Spencer, but miraculously, she kept quiet about the boys and her after dinner dime. Finally, the last plate was clean.

"Thanks for the great dinner, Mrs. Johnson." Alex and Zach

shared the compliment. Indigestion might have been a predictable outcome from the way the boys gobbled their food.

"Yeah, it was really super," said Tank, wiping spaghetti sauce off his chin and licking his milk mustache. He kept glancing at Spencer searching for some signal that it was okay to leave the table.

"Well, thank you, boys. I appreciated the good manners you boys showed, too." Spencer's mother stood up, ready to leave the table.

"Not so fast, guys. After you gentlemen help clear the table, you can be excused," said Dad.

Spencer looked at the boys and shrugged his shoulders. "Let's do this fast," he whispered.

They cleared the table at warp-speed, avoiding any breakage of dinner ware.

"Come on. Back to my room, guys," said Spencer. "The suspense is killing me!"

Chapter 9
Discovered

The boys bolted for Spencer's room and found the door open. Amy was sitting on Spencer's bed, her little arms folded across her chest, legs dangling. Her dark eyes flashed. She stuck out her lower lip and tried to look cross.

"Where's my dime, Spence? You promised after dinner, I get a dime, and I been waiting all nice," said Amy.

"Geez, Amy," said Tank. "What's the rush? You'll get your money."

"I want my dime now," said Amy, "or I'm telling Mamma you guys got Ellie's secret writing book."

The boys stopped short and stared at Amy. Their mouths hung open in disbelief. Their eyes widened to the point of popping.

"You should have hid the book, Spence." Alex whispered through clenched teeth. "Now what're we gonna do? Amy'll blab everything."

"How do you know that's Ellie's book, Amy?" Spencer was still reeling from his sister's discovery and pretended like it was no big deal.

"She showed me it when I was over to her house with Mamma one day," said Amy. "Ellie writes 'portant stuff and special secrets in it. She tol'me so. How come you got it? She borrowed it to you?"

"No Amy. She didn't *borrow* it to us. We *found* it, and we're going to give it back to her soon as we can." Spencer stretched the truth and tried to build a convincing case his five year old sister might buy.

"But you can't tell Ellie we have it, Amy. She would be very upset. It would hurt her feelings real bad. Understand? Her special secrets and stuff?" Spencer waited for some kind of response, but Amy just glared at him and the other three boys.

"Geez, Spence," whispered Tank, "what did ya say that for? Yer getting' us in deeper and deeper."

"Not to worry, guys. I think I can handle this," said Spencer confidently.

"Amy, how 'bout I give you TWO dimes? Until we get Ellie's secret book back to her, you got to promise not to tell anyone we have it. That'll be *our* secret. Just between you and us guys. Can you do that? It's nobody's business but *ours*. Okay?"

"Two dimes?" Amy was counting again. "As many as two fingers?" she asked.

"Right. That's like twenty pennies," said Spencer, hoping that twenty was a big enough number to keep her quiet.

"Okay, but when do I get 'em? Twenty pennies is a whole bunch! All my fingers and toes!"

"Right again, Amy. I have 'em right here in my bank. Let's count 'em out just for you," said Spencer. "I'll give you one dime and ten pennies. Together that makes twenty cents. Okay?" The bargain was made and together Spencer and Amy counted out the coins—one dime and ten pennies.

"Remember, Amy. It's got to be *our very important secret*. Don't tell anyone."

"Okay," said Amy. "Cross my heart. Promise." She skipped away to fill her own piggy bank.

"Okay, genius," said Zach. "That was possibly the stupidest thing you ever did. We can't trust Amy to keep her big mouth shut. How long do you think that'll last?"

"Long enough for us to read the diary, pick up some ideas, and get it back to Ellie before she knows we got it. But I still haven't figured out *how* to return it," said Spencer. "We got to think of something."

"Makes me nervous just having it now that Amy knows," said Alex. "Let's see what it says and get it over with."

"Here goes nothin'," said Spencer. "Shoot. According to this page, Becca has a crush on me. Sheesh! It says here, I'm brainy and cute. There's even a heart with our names on it. Gag."

"Geez, Spence. Looks like you got a girlfriend," said Tank.

"On the other hand, Ellie thinks I'm a big nerd. Get this. We *all* dress like fools. We're dorky and goofy . . ." Spencer read on.

"Zach, you're MR. ATHLETE, in capital letters, see? But, you're not as cool as Mia. Alex, you draw really good. And guess what? Ellie thinks *you're* cute. She wishes you would notice her, but you won't ever talk to her. Here's something about trashing our stuff at the river, and . . ."

"What about me? Anything about me in there?" asked Tank.

"Well, yeah as a matter of fact there is. In big fat letters Ellie writes:

"*I HATE TANK!!!!*—with four exclamation marks. *He's a BIG BLABBER MOUTH who has no manners and eats Twinkies for lunch. He even looks like a big giant Twinkie!!*"

"Geez, that's cold," said Tank. "For her information, I can't stand her either, Miss Fancy Pants, Ellie Covington. What'd I ever do to her? I just won't talk to her ever again. Let's rip the page out!"

"Take it easy, Tank," said Alex. "We have to give this back, remember?" *That was really a rotten thing for Ellie to write. Maybe Spence shouldn't of read that.*

The boys read into the evening, and then tried to come up with some kind of a plan to get the diary back to Ellie.

"I got nothin'," said Zach. "How 'bout you, Alex?"

"Nothin' here either. But I can't believe Ellie likes me. Now I won't even be able to look at her straight. Too embarrassing."

"Well, I can't believe Ellie HATES me so dang much!" said Tank. "Told ya I need to get me a life. How can anyone hate me? I'm a good guy. I'm cool. I think I'm nice."

"Guys, a plan? We need a plan," said Spencer. "How we gonna get this back to Ellie?"

Chapter 10
First Day Back to School—No Plan

The bus stop was crowded with a few anxious parents and lots of excited kids. Each sported something new to show off, and aside from the little tots who were clinging to their mothers, big kid talk centered on all the important issues. Who's going to be in what class, schedules, and what the cafeteria would be serving for lunch. Becca, Mia, and Ellie stood in one huddle, the boys in another, *with* Spencer's little sister, Amy.

"Geez, Spence," said Tank. "This is embarrassin'. A Kindergarten kid hanging out with us. Why can't she go with someone else?"

"You know I can't just dump her, Tank. Mom had to work today, and I promised I'd get Amy to the right class. Mom's already met the teacher at orientation or somethin'."

"But, Amy's been here a bunch of times with us guys." Tank frowned. "She knows the school."

"I know," said Spencer. "I'm just making sure she knows where she's supposed to go. At least she won't be sitting with us on the bus."

Trying to appear separate from the commotion around them,

Ellie, Becca, and Mia stayed in a close circle discussing their own personal agenda and all of Ellie's new school stuff.

"Did you guys get to see the class list yet?" asked Mia. "Think all of us will be together again this year?"

"Don't know," said Becca. "It'd be our luck to have to be with *those* guys yet again." She nodded in the boys' direction. Amy jumped up and down and waved to the girls.

"Maybe they'll grow up this year." Ellie laughed.

"Fat chance," said Mia. "They're too pea brained. They only care about sports and food."

"But they keep looking at us, and smiling," said Ellie. She waved back to Amy. "It's really creeping me out. Those dorks are probably planning something again."

"Ignore 'em, Ellie," said Becca, adjusting her glasses. "I guess they don't have anything better to do than stare at us. Just turn around, and don't look at 'em."

Amy ran off to talk to a friend who was waiting for the bus, too, and left the boys alone. With Amy gone, the boys' conversation kept coming back to the same topic. Ellie's diary. Especially now. Now that Ellie was standing in plain sight with Mia and Becca.

"How we going to get Ellie's diary back to her?" asked Alex. "Should we just pretend we found it? Or not give it back at all like Zach said? Like it just disappeared or something?"

"Maybe," said Zach. "We really got some good stuff to blackmail the girls with, but then we get ourselves to BIG trouble when they figure out our information didn't just fall out of the sky."

"Hold on guys," said Spencer. "There's no hurry. When the time is right, the diary will magically reappear. It's safe at home."

"Hidden this time I hope," said Tank. "You got somethin' in mind, Spence?"

"I think so."

"How about lettin' us in on it?" asked Alex.

"In good time, my man. In good time," said Spencer. "Cool it. Here comes the bus. We can talk later. Get over here, Amy. You got to sit in the front with the other little kids."

"Cut the yakking, girls. Here's the bus," said Mia. "How 'bout we get to the end of the line—behind the boys. That way maybe we can sit in back of them and eavesdrop. Catch some of their stupid conversation so you can write . . . Hey, Ellie? Did you ever find your diary?"

"Nope. That's a complete mystery. I had so many secrets about me, about us in it. I would be *so* embarrassed if anyone read it. I've looked everywhere. It just plain disappeared." *Maybe Rufus buried it. That would be safe. At least he can't read.*

"That's disastrous," said Becca. "You had it at the party, because you were reading stuff to us."

"Right," said Ellie. "But, it's just vanished into thin air."

Everyone got on the bus, found a place to sit, and held onto backpacks and books. The bus rumbled on and stopped a few more times before lumbering up the hill toward Lemon Grove Elementary. The constant hum of chattering students was suddenly interrupted.

"Cry-min-eee!" Mia said it with such force she practically lifted out of her seat. Everyone turned around and stared at her. Rosa, the bus driver slowed the bus and checked her mirror.

"Mia! For heaven's sake. Have you lost your mind? What's wrong with you?" Becca tried to divert attention away from Mia's sudden outburst.

"Ellie," said Mia in a more subdued voice, "you had your diary when we were spying on the boys at the river. I thought you might want to write stuff. Remember? You don't suppose . . ."

"You think I lost it there? I couldn't have. How?"

"Could it have gotten mixed up with the boys' stuff when we trashed their things?" Becca could hardly imagine the thought.

"Ohhhhh, man," moaned Ellie. "I'm dead! That's why the guys are staring at us. They found my diary. They must have found my diary. And you can bet they've read it!

This is THE most humiliating day of my life! How can I ever face anyone again? THEY'VE BEEN READING MY SECRET STUFF!"

Ellie was now so angry that if possible, her eyes would have burned holes in back of the boys' heads. Her face took on a look that unmistakably read: *Don't mess with me if you want to live!*

"Now what am I going to do, Becca?" asked Ellie, her blood at a boiling point. "Any ideas, Mia? You're always the one with the BIG ideas."

"Ellie," said Mia, "get a grip. You look like, well, like a mad dog. You're practically foamin' at the mouth. We'll think of somethin'. Meantime, fake it. Pretend you don't know anything. We'll figure somethin' out."

"It had better be soon or I am going to totally explode!" said Ellie. She thought about all the things she had written in her diary and wished for another planet to escape to.

At last the school bus rolled to a stop in front of the school. As the children got off, they were greeted by the Principal, Mrs. Matthews, and a small group of teachers who were helping students locate their classrooms. A few parents huddled around the office windows where the class lists were posted. Students bumped each other and pushed in closer to locate their names on the grade-level rosters.

"Shoot, you guys. Life couldn't get any worse," said Ellie. "We're in the *same* class with those jerks again. Wouldn't you know it? Room 10—Mrs. Gunderson. I am SO embarrassed." *How can I face Alex? He knows. I'm going to die.*

"Well, try to stay calm, Ellie," said Becca, sliding her glasses back to the bridge of her nose. "We'll stick together and get to the bottom of this."

"Right, Ellie," said Mia. "Play dumb. Don't let on you suspect anything. Let's sit by each other when we get in the classroom, *away* from those nerds. And for heavens sake, Ellie, don't look at 'em."

Chapter 11
Greetings Room 10

"Good morning everyone." There was a short pause while the class settled. "Welcome. I'm Mrs. Gunderson, your fifth-grade teacher. We will be having a full and exciting year with lots of hard work—but lots of fun, too. I'm sure you'll all want to be up for the challenge."

Little does she know. Ellie was deep in thought. *I hope* ***she's*** *up to the challenge. Spencer and company'll probably give her a melt-down. They've ruined my life."*

"Miss Covington? Ellie?" The teacher was taking roll. "Is that how you wish to be addressed?" asked Mrs. Gunderson.

"What? Oh, sorry Mrs. Gunderson. I was thinking of something else. Yes, Ellie's fine. Thank you."

Mrs. Gunderson had already called other names: Rebecca Bailey; Zachariah Brown, Susan Butterfield. She continued in a voice pleasant enough to hide the demanding reputation she'd earned from past years' students.

"Gerald Dietz?"

"Here."

"Megan Flannigan?"

She continued through the alphabetical list.

"Spencer Johnson?"

"Present. My friends call me Spence though."

"Thank you. Spence it is."

Next it was Mia's turn. Mrs. Gunderson studied Mia's name for a moment and looked up. "I'm not too sure if this is correct, so please help me get it right," said Mrs. Gunderson. "Mia . . . su . . . sha, Mat . . . suz . . . aki. Miasusha Matsuzaki. Is that correct?"

"Wow, Mrs. Gunderson! You got it the first time! But you can just call me Mia."

"THAT will be no problem, Mia," said Mrs. Gunderson. "What a lovely musical name."

"Thanks," said Mia. She smiled.

"Alejandro Medina?"

"Here, but I like Alex for short."

The Meyer twins were followed by the names of other students on the class list. Near the end was the name that gave Ellie a prickly shiver.

"Bradley Tankarian?"

"I'm here, but could ya call me Tank? That's what everybody calls me. I don't really like the name Bradley. Too uppity if ya know what I mean," said Tank not really telling the truth.

"I'll certainly consider that, Brad, I mean Tank. Give me time to remember," said Mrs. Gunderson. By the end of the list, thirty names had been called.

"I wonder what she'll do to us," whispered Becca.

"I don't know," Ellie whispered back. "Everyone thinks she's really tough. Mean even. I hope we *survive*!"

"That's the challenge," said Mia.

"Girls? Enough chatter," said Mrs. Gunderson. "I'm perfectly willing to let all of you sit where you have currently chosen, but I *will* rearrange the seating if too much conversation interferes with our learning. Does everyone understand?"

Yeses and okays echoed around the classroom as the students acknowledged Room 10's *talking* expectations.

Just wait, thought Ellie. *She hasn't tangled with stupid Tank yet. That blabber-mouth. I bet it doesn't take long before he's in the principal's office. Ooooooo, I could just scream.*

"Okay then. You can call me Mrs. 'G' if you like. Mrs. Gunderson is a real mouthful too. *Almost* as difficult as Mia's name!" She teased and smiled at Mia.

"Maybe she's okay after all," whispered Mia, "and she's not an old fossil like some kids said."

"Shh," said Becca. "You're gonna get us in trouble."

The usual first day speech was completed, and it was nearly lunch time. Mrs. Gunderson was about to begin the long list of fifth-grade requirements, assignments, and activities when there was a little knock at the door. It opened slowly.

Standing big as life in the doorway was AMY.

Uh, oh. This can't be good, thought Spencer.

Chapter 12
The Jig Is Up

"Well, hello, dear. Are you lost?" asked Mrs. Gunderson.

"No," said Amy. "I'm going to go home on the big yellow bus now. Number 3, 'cuz my Kinder-day is over, but I have to give Ellie's secret book to Spencer. He's my brother, you know. He losted it under his bed. He's 'posed to give it back to Ellie, but he forgot it, so I put it in my back-pack. Here Spence. I helped. I got the book for you. Now you can give it back to Ellie. I forgot to give you it at the bus stop. You can say thank you later. 'Bye!"

Amy smiled and handed the book to Mrs. Gunderson, waved at Spencer, and skipped off.

Spencer's face turned an ashen, greenish-white. He looked as though he had seen a ghost. *Don't look at Ellie. Don't look at Ellie.* His mind whirled.

Tank, Zach and Alex sat stiff as boards, glued to their seats, staring straight ahead. They didn't dare take their eyes off Mrs. Gunderson.

Geez, Spence, thought Tank, *some hiding place. Glad you don't hide money. I knew Amy couldn't be trusted. There goes our ammunition! And I'll be grounded again for sure. Shoooot.*

"Spencer? Spencer is this true?" asked Mrs. Gunderson. "Come up and get Ellie's book. Sounds pretty urgent that she get it back. How nice of your little sister to drop it by for you. You can give it back to Ellie now if you like." *There must be more to this story,* thought Mrs. Gunderson.

Spencer walked up to the front of the room and took the diary. *I feel a massive Ellie-storm coming on,* thought Spencer, *and there's nowhere to hide. Thanks a lot, Amy. I'll be living in an altered state when Dad finds out about this.*

Ellie walked halfway up the aisle. She looked as though she were about to laugh and cry at the same time. She held out one hand to take the diary from Spencer. The other was in a white-knuckled fist behind her back.

In a wickedly sarcastic voice Ellie said, "Thank you, Spencer. I certainly hope you took good care of it while you had it." *You weasel. Just wait!*

Spencer weakly choked out, "Um, you're welcome, Ellie."

Ellie turned to walk back to her desk and gave each of the boys her most menacing look. There was not a doubt in anyone's mind, she was fighting mad.

"Cool it, Ellie," whispered Mia. "You got the diary back. Don't blow it. Check it out. The guys are squirming like worms on a hook."

"Yeah, but now they know everything, Mia. Ev-er-y-thing," whispered Ellie. "We have NO MORE SECRETS. They'll ruin me. Ruin us."

"Wanna bet?" said Becca. She cupped her hand around her mouth. "I'll tell you something at lunch *nobody* knows. Not even Spence."

"And," Mia whispered, "how much do you wanna bet the guys will ask us for a deal? Keep the whole thing quiet so *they* don't get in trouble? Just wait."

"Once more, girls. Watch the talking, please," said Mrs. Gunderson more firmly. "Let's break for lunch everyone."

Chapter 13
Revelation

Lunch was the usual fare—boring. The three girls found a spot away from the confusion of old-timers and new students who were exchanging food, comparing teachers, and trying to find old friends.

"Let's sit here," said Ellie. "I don't see those fools anywhere. I can't face them anyway. Wish I could just disappear. I'm ruined." *Stupid, stupid, stupid jerks.*

"So what's this big secret, Becca?" asked Mia. "Must be pretty awesome."

"Well," said Becca, "I think it could be *very* big. You know how Tank always gets in trouble? How he hangs out at Spencer's house all the time?"

"That knucklehead," said Ellie. "He's been acting so weird lately. Even more than usual."

"Think I know why," said Becca, "but, maybe I shouldn't be telling anybody this. Daddy would have a fit if he knew I was telling."

Becca's father was the Reverend Timothy Bailey, Minister of River View Chapel—the little neighborhood church.

"Ah, *come on*," said Mia. "Don't do this to us. Tell us. We deserve something special. Can't be all that bad, can it?"

"Well, Mrs. Tankarian came over to the church the other day to talk to Daddy about Tank's father," said Becca.

"Tank's father?" The girls sang out in unison.

"Yeah, Tank's father," said Becca. She adjusted her glasses. "I guess he's been in jail for a long time."

"No way!" said Mia. "Tank said his dad was dead."

"Yeah, that's what he *told* us," said Becca. "I think he was trying to hide the fact his dad was in jail. Must really get to him."

"And?" said Ellie. "What else?"

"Tank's dad's name is Bradley. That's probably why Tank doesn't like to be called Brad—jail and all," said Becca. "I was just walking by Daddy's office, and I could hear him and Tank's mom talking. Thought I might find out something juicy about Tank, but I didn't expect to hear about his dad."

"Why was his dad in jail?" asked Mia.

"I'm not sure, but it sounded like he did something really bad. Now he's about to get out, and Mrs. Tankarian is worried how Tank's going to handle it," said Becca. "She seemed really upset. I guess his dad wasn't nice to her either."

"Then what?" asked Ellie.

"That's all I know," said Becca. "But if it was something really scary, it's no wonder Tank acts like he does. Daddy told Tank's mom to talk to the principal or something. Let his teacher know what's happening, too."

"You mean all this time his dad was in jail, and he just didn't tell anyone? That's ugly," said Mia. "I'd feel really rotten if my dad was in jail. Maybe we ought to go easy on Tank."

"If we go too easy, he'll get suspicious," said Becca. "Spencer's mom and dad probably know all about Tank's dad. Maybe that's why they practically let Tank *live* over at their house. Funny though. He never sleeps over. Wonder why?"

"Well, I for one *can't* let him off the hook for being such a stupid blabber mouth," said Ellie. *Sorry for Tank? I don't think so!*

"Shh!" said Becca. "Don't look now, but here comes Spence and Alex. No Zach and Tank though. Pretend we don't see 'em."

"I bet they want to make a deal, just like I said." Mia waited for their offer.

"You guys busy?" asked Spencer. "Sorry Amy dropped in with the diary drama like she did, Ellie. Didn't want that to happen."

"How DID you want it to happen, Spence? Now that you and your idiot friends have read every word of my personal business, you fools think you can get off the hook if I say, *Oh, that's all right. I know you didn't mean to.* Sure bet. Get real. What kind of a dope do you think I am anyway? Do I have STUPID written all over me?"

"Cool it, Ellie," said Mia. "You're gettin' all worked up again."

The boys backed up fearing Ellie might decide to take them out with a left hook.

"Ellie, give 'em a chance to say what they want," whispered Becca. "We can figure out a really good pay-back."

"Ellie, I . . ." Alex began an apology.

"Oh, SHUT up all of you!" said Ellie. "I don't want to talk about it. Anyway, there goes the bell, and I need time to think. Here comes your other partners in crime. They're prob'ly cooking something up, too."

At Room 10, Mrs. Gunderson stood in the doorway and directed the students to their seats. Then she picked up the year's-work conversation without skipping a beat.

"So class, aside from all the normal fifth-grade requirements, we'll be working on reports, taking field trips, working on a play, raising money for outdoor camp, and participating in the Science Fair and talent show."

"Cool," whispered Spencer. "Maybe she's not so bad after all."

A buzz from the intercom interrupted the class. *"Sorry to bother you, Mrs. Gunderson, but would you please send Zach Brown and Brad Tankarian to the office? Principal Matthews would like to see them."*

Well, that didn't take long, thought Ellie. *Trouble already?*

"First day of school and an office visit?" said Mrs. Gunderson. "I hope this isn't anything serious, boys. Not a good way to start off the year. You'll be without field trips and camp if this continues." They nodded and left the room.

"Have a chair, boys," said Mrs. Matthews. "I've been told that the two of you had some kind of a problem on the playground at lunch recess. Care to tell me about it? I'm really surprised at you, Tank. I thought we agreed that your behavior was going to improve this year."

"Yeah, I know, but Zach called me a pansy or some kinda dumb flower. Made me mad, so I pushed him—not hard or nothin'—just kidding, but he pushed me back, so I pushed him again," said Tank. "Then he fell on his elbow."

"And what's your story, Zach? Not like you to be in my office," said Mrs. Matthews. "I thought you boys were friends."

"We are," said Zach. "I mean we were. Prob'ly shouldn't of said what I did, but Tank's actin' weird. He don't want to play soccer or basketball or nothin'. He just messes around and pushes everybody if he don't get his way."

The usual principal conversation continued with the apology, the writing assignment, and the dreaded phone call home. "Don't let this happen again, boys, or we'll have more than a phone call to worry about. Got it?" said Mrs. Matthews. "Now back to class with you. I'll be expecting your writing tomorrow first thing." Zach and Tank shook hands and returned to class.

"Geez, Zach," said Tank. "Wish you wouldn't of got so mad. I was just jokin'. Now Mom's gonna ground me. Be lucky if I *ever* get to leave the house this whole year. And I *don't* wanna get stuck there."

"You really been actin' strange, Man. Not like you to be so pushy. Somethin' got ya?"

"Nah, I'm okay."

The principal watched the boys head for their class. She closed her door and picked up the phone. "Mrs. Tankarian? This is Principal Matthews."

Chapter 14
Getting It Right

When Tank and Zach got back to the classroom, Mrs. Gunderson was in the middle of more instructions.

"First assignment for all of you," said Mrs. Gunderson, "is to write a short biographical sketch about yourself and then draw a self portrait for Back to School Night. Your bios tell me a lot—your likes and dislikes—your talents—your family. I'll pass out mirrors so you can look at yourself while you draw. First, however, you write."

Cheers and groans followed as the students began the writing task. Some biographies were no surprise:

"My dad works for the county . . . Mom is a nurse . . . I live with my grandma . . . We have horses and dogs . . ." But Mrs. Gunderson was particularly struck by Tank's writing.

"I am 10 and a haf. I live with my mom. My grammas live far away. I don't got any pets. My mom works. We don't hardly go nowhere but the store and my soccer games. Sometimes I get mad that I ain't got a real dad—I mean the kind that sticks around and comes to games and stuff. Guess I got a dad somewhere. I don't egzackly know where

he is. Mom don't talk about him. He went away when I was little, so I tell everybody he died. Spencer's dad is good. I like him. He is nice. I think my dad might not be good."

Mrs. Gunderson looked up from Tank's paper. *I think a call to Tank's mom might be in order. Maybe Mrs. Matthews can shed some light on this, too.*

The drawing part of the assignment drew fits of laughter and groans of frustration. Mrs. Gunderson relaxed the rules while the class painstakingly tried to create exact images of themselves.

"Double darn. I can't do this!" exclaimed Ellie. "I'm not in the mood. All I can think about is my diary and those stupid idiots."

"Looks like you know what you're doing, Ellie," said Mia. "I think it's nice."

"That's what *you* think," said Ellie. "My pony-tail looks like a witches' broom, and I look all cross-eyed. Look at my lips. They're like two big smashed beets. This is totally gross."

"Well, look at me," said Mia. "You'd think straight black hair and brown eyes would be easy, but my eyes look like peach pits. I can't make the ovals slant the right way, and my eyebrows look like one big fat slug. But, hey. That's as good as it's gonna get. I think Mom and Dad will recognize me."

"Well, I look like I have a brown bush on my head," said Becca. "My eyes look like my cat's when she's mad—green and skinny. I picked red for my glasses. At least *they* weren't hard to draw."

"You even got 'em hangin' off your nose like usual. When you gonna get those things fixed?" asked Mia.

"I'll ignore that," said Becca. "At least I got my nose where it's *supposed* to go, even if the glasses are hanging."

The boys examined their efforts too. "Brownish, yellowish short hair and blue eyes. Is that how I look?" asked Spencer. "Yours is cool, Zach. Black hair and all. You even got the right brown for your skin."

"I can live with it," said Zach. "It's cool."

Tank colored curly red hair on his head, made blue eyes, and a flock of freckles. Some were like dots and others like *who cares* mistakes.

Alex hovered over his portrait.

"Geez, Alex, how can you do that so good? Really looks like you," said Tank. "Looks like your brothers, too."

"Duh, Tank," said Alex. "I'm Mexican? Everybody I know from there has dark hair and brown eyes. I'd draw all day if the teacher would let me."

"Bet you'll be famous some day," said Tank. "Don't know if I'll be anything—ever."

That's a dumb thing to say, thought Spencer. He glanced at Zach and Alex. They just shrugged their shoulders.

The students were so engrossed in their drawing activity that they didn't notice a student slip into the classroom and hand a note to Mrs. Gunderson.

"Okay, kids," said Mrs. Gunderson. "Look at the time. We have to wrap it up for today. Our first day back being a Friday will allow you the whole weekend to think about this year and all our upcoming projects. Tank, could you stay after school for a few minutes? I'd like to talk to you."

"But, I take the bus, Mrs. 'G'," said Tank.

"Hey, we don't *have* to take the bus, Tank," said Spencer. "Us guys'll wait for you. We can all walk home together. Okay if we wait outside, Mrs. 'G'?"

"Sure," said Mrs. Gunderson. "We won't be long, boys. Class dismissed. See you all Monday. Have a nice weekend everyone."

The students moved quickly out of Room 10 and left Mrs. Gunderson and Tank alone. "I read your biography, Tank," said Mrs. Gunderson, "and I was somewhat concerned that perhaps you may have something bothering you about your dad. I'm here to listen if you need someone to talk to."

"Thanks, Mrs. 'G'," said Tank, "but I don't got anythin' to say. Leastwise, I don't think I got anythin' to say. Nothin' important. Mom's kinda sad lately. Like she's thinkin' about somethin'. I can't figure it. Maybe I done somethin'."

"Well, just before school got out, Principal Matthews sent me a note," said Mrs. Gunderson. "She spoke with your mom about today's playground incident, and your mom wants to talk with us Monday after school—you included, of course."

"I ain't got a problem with that," said Tank. "She gonna talk about me? Am I getting' s'pended? Prob'ly grounded again, huh?"

"Whatever it is Tank, I'm sure we'll be able to talk it through and come up with some kind of solution," said Mrs. Gunderson. "Okay?"

"Yeah," said Tank. "Know I'm grounded though. No gettin' around that. That always happens. See ya Monday."

"Okay, Tank," said Mrs. Gunderson. "And Tank? I *did* remember to call you Tank. I'm learning, too."

"Thanks, Mrs. 'G'. See ya later."

"What was that all about?" asked Spencer. "You in some kind of trouble?"

"Maybe," said Tank. "I guess Ma's comin' to talk to Mrs. 'G' and the principal Monday, and she wanted me to know about it. Prob'ly gettin' grounded again. Let's not talk about it, okay?"

"Okay by me," said Alex. "Come on. We can take the bike trail. The girls took the bus. Bet we beat 'em home. And no homework tonight. YA-HOO!"

Chapter 15
The Big Mistake

The bike trail meandered downhill from Lemon Grove Elementary to the small River View neighborhood. The foursome did some walking and a little jogging as they headed home. Now and then they chatted. Mostly about nothing. Sometimes about Amy and *THE DIARY* —a little about the office visit.

"I dread going home," said Spencer. "You think *you're* grounded, Tank? When my dad finds out we read Ellie's diary and kept it all this time, he'll probably make me stay in for a month, and I'll have to scrub the floor with a toothbrush!"

"That's kinda extreme, don't ya think?" asked Zach. "I'm saying nothin'. Not one word. Maybe I'll be lucky and escape gettin' grounded."

"Don't count on it," said Alex. "Our parents talk. It'll just be a matter of time, and I'll be doin' double chores for everybody."

At the bottom of the hill, the trail took off in another direction. So the boys left the bike path and walked along the side of the two-lane road, their backs to the traffic.

"You're awful quiet, Tank," said Spencer. "What's up?"

"Just thinkin' how stupid me and Zach were. Shouldn't a happened. Trouble I mean," said Tank.

"What'd you guys do anyways?" asked Alex.

"Ah, we were just playin' around, and I grabbed the ball from Zach. He called me some stupid name, so I shoved him. Easy, like this." Tank gave Spencer a friendly shove. "Then Zach pushed me back harder," said Tank.

"Yeah, I let him have a good one," said Zach. "No big deal, but I guess Tank thought it was too much."

"Yeah. So I pushed again, and Zach fell, kinda hard," said Tank.

The boys began a friendly push and shove game while they were walking, but things got more physical and a little rough.

"Cut it out, Zach! Said I was sorry!" Tank was getting angry.

They were so involved in their pushing game that none of them heard the car coming up behind them. It was too late. Zach's shove was just enough. Alex and Spencer grabbed for Tank and missed his hand.

Tires squealed and brakes smoked. Close by, Old Man Potter, hands full of junk from a recent trash collection, jerked his head up and saw the tragedy unfold. He dropped everything, ran toward the black SUV, and the boy lying in a crumpled heap on the ground in front of it.

"Call 911!" the old man hollered to the driver. He knelt down and leaned over the youngster with the red curly hair and whispered. "Can you hear me, son? Don't move. Help is coming." Potter kept whispering softly to Tank and placed his weathered hands over the gaping red wound on Tank's twisted leg. "Hang in there, son. It'll be okay."

The hysterical driver handed her phone to someone in the gathering crowd. She stared at the child in front of her car and wept. Someone else put an arm around her.

Within minutes, the yellow school bus pulled up to its usual stop within view of the commotion. The students stood up to leave. However, Rosa, the driver, didn't open the door.

"What's going on?" yelled Mia. "What's everybody looking at?"

"All I can see is a big black car," said Becca. She adjusted her glasses. "Look over there! There's Spencer and Alex. They're crying. Zach is sitting on the ground. He's totally green like he's gonna throw up, and here comes Daddy running up the street."

"Where's Tank?" yelled Ellie. "Where's Tank?"

"Can't see him," said Mia, "but, there's Old Man Potter. He keeps bendin' over something."

"Think it's Tank, Mia?" asked Ellie. "Is it Tank?"

"Can't tell from here. Could be a dog maybe. Can we *please* get off the bus, Rosa?" asked Mia.

"Nope. You sit tight, girls," she said. "Too much confusion out there. You kids'll be better off in the bus. Wait for your folks to come get you."

"But, it might be Tank . . . hurt maybe . . . or worse. Please let us out!" begged Ellie. Tears began to flow as the girls imagined the worst. The sound of fire trucks and an ambulance, their sirens blaring, rushed onto the scene followed by a couple of squad cars.

"Take it easy, girls," said Rosa. "I'll radio the dispatcher and see if I can get any information." *I hope to God it's not . . . I hope no one got killed.* Rosa tapped her fingers.

"Please hurry!" cried Mia, jumping up and down. "There's

Tank's mom, and Spencer's dad," said Becca. "Daddy's got his arm around Zach now. What do you think happened?"

The younger children on the bus crowded toward the front and began to cry.

"I'm still waiting for an answer," said Rosa. *Hurry up down there. Hurry up!* "The dispatcher is checking. In the meantime girls, try to comfort the little guys. They're pretty scared. I need to listen for directions."

Ellie turned around with Becca and they began talking to the children. Paramedics opened the back of the ambulance, slid out the gurney, and moved in next to the firemen who were already administering first aid.

"Can you see anything?" asked Becca. She patted a little boy who was crying.

"Nope," said Mia, "too many people now. Maybe when everyone moves out of the way I'll catch what's going on."

"Look over there!" said Becca. "I've never seen that guy before. He's walking over to Tank's mom. Could be a doctor. Or maybe Tank's dad. You think?"

"Heck if I know," said Mia. "Wouldn't know him if I saw him anyway, but Spencer's dad's takin' Alex and Spence with him."

"Please, Rosa, please let us off the bus." Ellie was panicked .

Parents were now at the door of the bus asking for their kids. Rosa signed them off one by one until only the three girls were left.

"Over and out." Rosa spoke to the dispatcher and clicked off the radio. *Thank God!* "Okay, girls, listen up. We're not getting off the bus. Tank *is* the one who got hurt. He'll be okay, but I guess his leg is broken and he's pretty banged up. If it hadn't been for Old Man Potter, well let's just say it's a darn good thing Potter got there when he did."

"Where'd Mr. Potter go?" asked Ellie. "I don't see him anywhere. Maybe he saved Tank's life. We need to find him."

Ellie's dad rushed up to the bus. "I'll take the girls from here, Rosa," said Mr. Covington. "Mia and Becca will be at our house until things get sorted out. Call me if you get any more details." He ushered the protesting girls away from the accident and to his van.

"Thanks, Mr. Covington. I'll let Becca's dad know you have her with you. Looks like he'll be tied up for awhile," said Rosa.

"Thanks, Rosa."

Ellie's eyes filled with tears as she and the girls climbed into the van. She looked through the back window and watched Tank being lifted into the ambulance. His mother reached out to hold his hand. The strange man was walking away from the ambulance. "Who *is* that guy, Dad?"

"That'd be Tank's father. Seems he just got to town after being away for some time."

"Yeah, jail," whispered Ellie. "You were right Becca. But somehow I know this is all my fault," she sobbed.

"You can't be serious, Ellie," said Becca, looking over the top of her glasses. "How do you figure that one? You're way off there."

"Nope," said Ellie, "I've been really mean to Tank. I just know it's all my fault! Now I'm being punished."

"Everything okay back there?" Ellie's dad could hear some of the agitated conversation. "Who's crying?"

Chapter 16
Now What?

Zach collapsed in Reverend Bailey's arms and sucked in a rattling breath of air; his sobs erupting in irregular patterns of grief and disbelief.

"Zach, no one could have predicted this would happen," said Reverend Bailey. He pulled his arm tighter around Zach. "It was an accident. A terrible accident. Everyone knows you boys would never intentionally hurt each other. We'll get through this."

"Where's my mom?" sobbed Zach. "I want my mom."

"She's on her way. She'll be here real soon," said Reverend Bailey. "But, I think I see Principal Matthews coming."

"I don't wanna talk to her. I don't wanna talk to anybody. I just want my mom!" Zach was emotionally spent. His eyes were swollen and red from crying. "I'm already in enough trouble. I think I'm going to puke."

Reverend Bailey looked up as Mrs. Matthews arrived and shook his head.

"Mr. Feldon, our school counselor is on his way, Reverend," said Mrs. Matthews. "You can fill him in on the details. I'll take care of talking with Zach's mother. Have you heard from her yet?"

"As a matter of fact, I think I see her," said Reverend Bailey.

That's all Zach heard. 'I think I see her'. He jumped up, ran to his mother, fell into her arms and cried.

"I didn't mean to hurt Tank, Mamma. We were just kiddin' around, and I pushed too hard, and the car hit him. I tried to grab Tank. I didn't mean to, I didn't mean to." He buried his head in his mother's arms and sobbed. "Is he going to die? Please tell me he's not going to die! I don't want him to die! He's my friend!"

"Zach, honey, hold on," said his mother. She stroked his head. "Take a deep breath. Easy now. Tank's *not* going to die. He's hurt, but he won't die. This was a terrible, terrible thing to have happened to you boys. Could just as easily have been you, you know, Zach. You boys get too rambunctious sometimes and forget all about everything but having fun."

"Excuse me, Mrs. Brown." Mrs. Matthews interrupted softly. "I am so sorry about this whole thing. I just wanted you to know that our counselor, and the nurse, and Reverend Bailey will be at school Monday morning to talk with the kids about the accident. Just Mrs. Gunderson's class.

"Over the weekend, this incident will become full of misinformation and rumor. I think it would be good for Zach to be at school with all of us. You too, please, if you're able." Mrs. Matthews looked at both of them and wondered if they actually heard anything she had just said, and then she continued.

"We want to make sure that everyone knows how this situation could have been avoided, but more importantly, we want Zach to know he's not alone. It could have been so much worse. Tank's classmates will most likely want to do something to encourage

Tank, and I'll just bet Zach would like to be a part of that as well." She looked down at Zach's trembling figure, hoping to see some sign of relief.

"Mrs. Gunderson is at the hospital with Tank and his mother now. She'll up-date me as soon as she can, and I'll call you. Please, just think about it for now. Hard as this is, I believe it would be good for Zach to get himself back to school with his friends right away."

"Well, Mrs. Matthews, right now I just need to get Zach home. He's really shaken up. Probably in shock. But, I *will* give it some thought. Tank's mother must be very upset and angry, too. I would be," said Mrs. Brown. "Especially now that Tank's father is back in town."

"You *know* about Tank's father?" Mrs. Matthews shook her head. "Word sure gets around fast in this community. That's a whole other issue Tank has to deal with. He's really going to need our support more than ever."

Zach, emotionally exhausted, just leaned against his mother and stared at no one and nothing in particular. Now, more relaxed and wrapped in his mother's arms, he drooped like a rag doll.

"I've got to get Zach home, Mrs. Matthews. He's terribly traumatized. I'm going directly to his doctor as well. See what she says about how soon Zach should come back to school. I really appreciate your concern though."

"Can we please go see Tank, Mamma," Zach pleaded. "Please? I need . . . I want to talk to him. I *have* to talk to him."

"We'll wait to hear from Mrs. Gunderson, dear. Maybe tomorrow sometime. We need to be sure he can have company. Okay? Besides, I think Tank's father is there now. Come on. Let's go home."

Chapter 17
The Hospital

Brenda, Tank's mother, hardly able to digest the horror now confronting her, spoke in a wavering and choked voice.

"Thank you for being here, Mrs. Gunderson. This has to be the *worst* day of my life. Not only is Tank seriously hurt, but his father, shows up *today* of all days after being in jail for the past eight years. We've been divorced for some time, and I simply don't need any more problems, especially not now. He just took off a few minutes ago. Probably wandering around the hospital somewhere."

"Well, I'm here to do whatever I can to help you, Mrs. Tankarian," said Mrs. Gunderson. "Have you heard anything yet?"

"No. Call me Brenda, please. Tank's in the emergency room. They're getting him ready for surgery, and I was asked to leave. The doctor said he'd come and get me when they're done with x-rays. I'm so frightened, Mrs. Gunderson. I just can't believe this is happening."

Brenda paced the floor, reached across an elderly woman for the tissue box on the magazine table, and stared at the waiting room door.

"I can't think," she said, pacing the floor. "I just can't think right now."

Her eyes filled with tears. She reached for Mrs. Gunderson's hand and cried. "I hope Tank will be all right. He's such a good kid. I couldn't bear losing him. These boys can be so careless when they play. They just don't think . . ."

"Mrs. Tankarian?" A nurse opened the door to the emergency room. "You can come in now. Dr. Ellis will go over everything with you. We've given your son a sedative so he's resting more comfortably. Come on in."

X-rays clipped along a lighted wall made a gruesome mosaic of Tank's broken leg. A bag of something liquid hung from a metal pole. Clear plastic tubing dropped from the bag and ended abruptly in Tank's arm. Trays of gauze, scissors, and syringes rested on a table next to the bed. Tank's head was wrapped in bandages; his left eye black and swollen; his nose and lip scraped; eyes closed now. The smell of rubbing alcohol and disinfectant permeated the sterile room. Dr. Ellis held a clip-board in one hand and reached for Tank's mother with the other.

"Hello, Mrs. Tankarian. How are you doing? Holding up okay?"

"I'm trying," she said, dabbing a tissue at her eyes.

"Good. I know this is hard, but first of all I want you to know your son is going to be all right. He's pretty banged up, but I venture he'll be good as new with your care and a little time to heal. Let me show you what we've found in our examination, and then I'll need a signature from you so we can proceed with treatment."

"Tank has a slight concussion," said Dr. Ellis. "We've cleaned him up and stitched his forehead. Shouldn't leave a scar. He's got some pretty nasty abrasions on his face and arms. And as you can see in the x-rays here, his leg is broken in three places which will require surgery. That's what I will need from you—a signature on the consent form for surgery. Are you still with me?"

"Yes, but he looks so helpless and fragile just lying there," said Mrs. Tankarian. "Are you sure he's okay? May I please give him a kiss?"

"Of course," said Dr. Ellis. "I can assure you he's okay. Just pretty groggy from the sedative. It's important we get him into surgery right away though. I've called Tank's pediatrician, Dr. Beegle. She should be here soon. I expect we'll keep Tank here in the hospital for about a week, and if there are no complications, he can go home then. I understand his father is here. Do I need to speak with him?"

"No . . . um, no. I'll fill him in on everything. He really has nothing to do with us any more," said Mrs. Tankarian. "That's another story. Thank you, though, Dr. Ellis. Just one more kiss before you take him to the operating room. Where do I sign?"

Chapter 18
The Long Wait

Tank's mother left the emergency room, found a somewhat worn but comfortable chair in the waiting room and sat down, exhausted. Mrs. Gunderson was still waiting.

"You haven't gone home yet?" asked Brenda. "I think you've been more than helpful, Mrs. Gunderson. I wouldn't feel at all bad if you wanted to leave."

"I thought I'd stay awhile longer. Just 'til you feel more at ease. You must be hungry. Can I get you something?"

"I couldn't eat a thing, thanks, but I would like something to drink."

"Sure. I'd be happy to get you something, but before I go looking for a vending machine, I'd like to ask you a question."

"What's that?" asked Brenda. Her weary body sank deeper into the chair.

"While you were in the emergency room, I got a call from Principal Matthews. She's been with Zach's mother. I guess Zach is completely devastated by . . ."

"Well, he should be after what happened," interrupted Brenda.

There was definite anger in her voice. "Those boys should have been more careful walking along the street like that, pushing and shoving. Tank didn't have a chance."

"I don't blame you for being upset, Brenda, but would you be open to hearing what I learned?" asked Mrs. Gunderson. "I think it might help to know how all this unfolded, at least according to how Reverend Bailey explained it."

Before Tank's mother could answer, Dr. Beegle opened the waiting room door. She was preparing to assist Dr. Ellis in the operating room; her 'scrubs' almost complete; a paper towel crumpled in her hand; an elbow holding the door.

"Hello, Brenda," said Dr. Beegle. "Wanted to let you know I'm here. Got here as soon as I could. Zach's mother came into my office awhile ago and told me what happened to these kids today. I'm so sorry for all of you. I had to give Zach something to calm him down. He's a total wreck. Vomiting. Crying. He really wants to see Tank. I hope you might allow that. Tomorrow afternoon would probably be okay."

"Well, I don't . . ."

Dr. Beegle interrupted. "Awful as it seems, this isn't anyone's fault. Just a horrible accident. Meanwhile I need to get to the OR. I'll be back here to talk with you as soon as we're finished. Looks like Tank's going to do just fine. Nice you're here for Brenda, Mrs. Gunderson." Dr. Beegle turned and let the door swing closed behind her.

"How does she know you?" asked Brenda.

"School," was all Mrs. Gunderson said.

"Oh." Tank's mother was pulling everything together in her mind. "I guess maybe I should hear what you have to say, Mrs. Gunderson."

The outer waiting room door opened. Brad Tankarian was balancing a tray that held a sandwich and two cups of coffee.

"Thought you might need this," said Brad. "Have you heard anything yet?"

Brenda looked at Mrs. Gunderson and sighed. "Mrs. Gunderson, this is Tank's father, Brad. Brad, Mrs. Gunderson."

So this is the 'sometime' father Tank wrote about. "Hello," said Mrs. Gunderson. "Nice to meet you."

"Mrs. Gunderson is Tank's teacher," said Brenda. "She was just about to explain what happened today. Sit down. I'm sure we both need to hear this. Thanks for the coffee. Care for some, Mrs. Gunderson?"

"Thanks, no. I'm fine," she said, pulling up another chair. *Interesting. He didn't offer anything.* Mrs. Gunderson explained the sequence of events that led up to the hospital vigil.

"That's the story. I wish to heaven it would have turned out differently, but unfortunately and sadly, it didn't. Monday, morning, some of our school staff and Reverend Bailey are going to speak to the whole class. Be nice if you could join us. With your help and permission though, I have an idea. More of a surprise for the kids, including Tank. Are you interested in hearing me out?"

"Well," said Brenda, "we aren't going anywhere until Tank is out of surgery. What did you have in mind? That reminds me. I very much would like to thank that Mr. Potter is it? . . . for what he did to help Tank. Whatever happened to him anyway?"

"We're still looking for him," said Mrs. Gunderson. "At least we know where he lives. Shouldn't be too hard to locate him. Anyway, this is what I had in mind. After that, maybe you could tell me something about yourself, Brad."

He looked down at the floor, shrugged his shoulders, and offered no response.

Chapter 19
Something to Do

Saturday morning. Ellie jerked awake. *Nope. It wasn't a dream. It really happened.* Somewhere in the distance Ellie heard the phone ring. *Is it bad news? Please don't let it be bad news.*

"Ellie, dear. Telephone," Ellie's mom called upstairs. "It's Mia. She wants to talk to you."

Good. Nothing serious. Let's hope.

"Coming!" Ellie yawned, shoved her arms into her bathrobe, and plodded downstairs to the kitchen; her eyes red and puffy from too much crying and not enough sleep. She picked up the phone. "Hey, Mia. What's up?"

"You don't sound so good," said Mia. *"You okay?"*

"Not really. I kept having nightmares," said Ellie.

"Me too. I kept wakin' up and thinking about Tank all night," said Mia. *"I kept seein' him bein' pushed into that ambulance. Made me really sad. Anyway, I just talked to Becca. She said Spencer and Alex want us to come over to Spencer's house around eleven. Something about making a poster or a giant get well card for Tank. They're inviting us to help if we want. I'm goin'. So's Becca. You wanna come?"*

"Yeah," said Ellie. "Might be good to talk to the guys and find out the whole story. See how they're feeling, too. Alex'll probably have some good ideas for a card. Think Zach will be there?"

"Prob'ly not. Mom called Zach's mom and I guess he's really torn up. All he wants to do is go see Tank at the hospital."

"Well, I don't blame him. I feel rotten, too," said Ellie, "but I think I can get it together today. Be nice if we could all go see Tank."

"Yeah," said Mia. *"Mom's gonna call the hospital later. Maybe we'll know something then."*

"Hope so," said Ellie. "Anyway, guess I'll see you at Spencer's around eleven. 'Bye."

Ellie stared blankly at the phone. *If only I hadn't said all those terrible things about Tank. Maybe he would be okay.*

"Mom?" called Ellie. "Do we have any Twinkies?"

"Heavens, no," said Ellie's mom. She walked into the kitchen holding a cup of coffee. "Why do you want Twinkies? You weren't thinking of having those for breakfast were you?"

"No," said Ellie, "I just was thinking we could surprise Tank with a basket full of them. Take them to the hospital or something. Twinkies are his favorite. Prob'ly couldn't get them past the nurses though, even if we tried to sneak them in."

"Got that right," said Ellie's mom. "What did Mia want?"

"She said the kids are going over to Spencer's to work on a get well card and she wanted to know if I could come. Can I?"

"That's a marvelous idea. Maybe you'll feel better being with everyone. Of course you can go. I'll take you over whenever you're ready. Meantime, you need some breakfast, but I guarantee it won't be Twinkies!"

At Zach's house, it was much the same—a slow and depressing morning.

"How much longer do I have to wait, Mom?" asked Zach. "I really wanna see Tank."

"The nurse said by this afternoon Tank would probably be alert enough to take in a short visit," said Zach's mother. "And she did mean *short.* How are you feeling? You fell asleep on my lap last night."

"I'm okay, but I'll feel better after I see Tank. Think he'll be mad at me? How 'bout his mom? She gonna be mad at me?" asked Zach.

"I don't think so, dear. I talked with Mrs. Tankarian this morning. After Mrs. Gunderson and Dr. Beegle talked with her, she seemed to understand what happened. She wouldn't have wanted you to be hurt either. Lucky for all of us, you and Tank have the same doctor. She's been a big help to all of us."

"Can I take Tank a present when I go see him?" asked Zach. "He doesn't like to read much, so not a book. Well, maybe a comic book. How 'bout a toy? An electronic toy? Can we go to the store and look for something? Get him something maybe?"

"Why not?" said Zach's mother. "Let's go look for a get-well-really-quick something! I think it would cheer both of you up." *That's my boy! Finally. You're coming around.*

Chapter 20
The Biggest Card Ever

"Where did you get that gigantic piece of cardboard, Alex?" asked Ellie.

"My brother got it for us. He found it behind the appliance store down on Main Street. Must've been part of a huge freezer box. We have to paint it all white first, so it's nice and clean."

"Have an idea already? I mean, what you're going to draw?" asked Ellie. She tried to encourage some kind of conversation from Alex.

"Yep! I already made a sketch. Like it?" Alex handed the drawing to Ellie.

"Awesome, Alex! You made everyone in the class like a little cartoon, even Mrs. Gunderson."

"I like the way you spelled out 'WE MISS YOU' and 'GET WELL QUICK' in Twinkie shapes," said Becca. She slid her glasses to the bridge of her nose.

"Boy, Alex. That's some drawing," said Mia. "Think we can get it done in time? This looks like a lot of work."

"I think we can knock this out by Sunday," said Alex, "with you guys helping, of course. Then on Monday, we can have everyone sign it. Spencer's dad said he'd take it over to the hospital."

"*IF* he can get it through the door!" said Spencer, laughing. "This is gonna to be the biggest get well card I've ever seen."

"You guys get much sleep last night?" asked Mia.

"Couldn't," said Alex. "Kept seeing that black car."

"I had nightmares all night," said Spencer.

Mia yawned and reached around the boys for a paintbrush. "I sure didn't." She dipped the paintbrush into the white paint and slathered a wide splotch across the cardboard.

"I don't think any of us did," said Becca. "My dad was up almost all night talking to a whole bunch of people. Even to Tank's dad, I think. It was impossible to sleep." She picked up another piece of yellow paper.

"Well, I had nightmares, too. I think this whole thing is *my* fault," said Ellie. "Mom and Dad say it isn't, but I'm not sure."

"You got to be kidding," said Spencer. "Where'd you get a crazy idea like that?"

"You know. I've always given Tank a bad time," said Ellie, "because he's, well, because he's just Tank. And after he blabbed about my party, and you guys took my diary, and read all my stuff, I was really *steamed*. I had mean and ugly thoughts about Tank. About you guys too. I called him stupid, and blabber mouth, and fat Twinkie. You know. All that stuff. You think bad thoughts could make someone get hurt? Like maybe I put a spell on him or something?"

"Never heard of that before," said Alex. He sharpened his pencil. "You said you were mad at us too, but me and Spence are still here. Besides it didn't happen that way, Ellie. Us guys tried really hard to grab Tank, but we couldn't. How do you think *we* feel?

Zach and Tank were foolin' around when they shouldn't of been. I just keep wishing we could of been faster."

"Well, I made up my mind I'm going to be nicer to Tank," said Ellie. "Just in case I had something to do with the accident." Ellie traced five more Twinkie shapes and picked up a pair of scissors.

The card-makers kept the discussion going about Tank. They worked into the afternoon and managed to complete a lot of the design, but other obligations demanded their attention.

"That's the last paper Twinkie I ever want to see," said Becca. "I stacked them up in piles, Alex. One pile for each word. I got to get home now you guys. My brother's got a game today. Can I use your phone, Spence?"

"Sure, Becca."

"Want us to come back tomorrow, Spence?" asked Ellie.

"That'd be great. If we want this done by Monday, Alex'll need all of us to finish it. You staying, Alex?"

"Sure. Then I can finish my drawing."

"Dad told me to call when I was ready to come home," said Becca. "Mia? Ellie? We can drop you guys home if you want. I'm glad we got together. See you guys tomorrow, but it'll have to be *after* church for me."

"Maybe I'll go to church with you, Becca and say a little prayer for Tank," said Ellie.

"How 'bout Zach?" asked Mia. "Think he'll want to help us?"

"Spence and me can call him later," said Alex. "See how he's doing. Maybe he'd want to come over tomorrow, too."

"Good idea. Tomorrow then. 'Bye guys," said Becca. She headed for the phone with Mia and Ellie close behind.

That same afternoon, Zach and Mrs. Brown went to the hospital to see how Tank was recovering. The elevator door opened on the 3rd floor and they stepped out.

"It's Room 303," said Mrs. Brown. "This way, Zack. Now don't get too excited when you see Tank. Hospitals like things on the quiet side."

At Room 303, Zach peered around the large hospital-room door and searched for some movement from the motionless figure on the bed.

"Tank. Hey, Tank. It's me, Zach. Are you awake?" Zach whispered loud enough to rouse Tank's mother who was napping in a chair next to Tank's bed. She smiled and motioned for Zach and his mother to come into the room.

"Hello, Savanna. Hi, Zach. Are you feeling better, dear? Heard you've had a pretty rough time young man. Tank should be waking up soon. It's getting time for his meds again, and he's been asking for you."

"Brenda? Zach and I . . ." Savanna began to offer a sympathetic response.

"Please, don't," said Brenda. "Mrs. Gunderson explained the whole awful story. When I think of what could have happened, it makes me shudder. I just hope you boys have learned a big lesson."

"You bet, Mrs. Tankarian," said Zach. "I would never hurt Tank on purpose. We were just fooling around."

"Mom? Who's here?" Tank, still groggy from all the sedatives and medication he'd been given, woke up.

"It's me, Tank. It's me. I came to see how you're doin'."

"Geez, Zach. I was hopin' you'd come to see me," said Tank. "I sort of lost it after that last shove. Don't remember much else."

"So . . . then . . . does that mean . . . are you mad at me?" asked Zach.

"Nah. But I don't *ever* want to play that game again. It was really scary," said Tank. "We were stupid, Zach. No more shovin' games from now on, at least not on the street."

"Not **anywhere** if I have anything to say about it!" said Zach's mother.

"Well, I'm really, really, sorry, Tank," said Zach. He bit his lip to discourage the tears that were forming in his eyes. "I never wanted to hurt you."

Tank's mother got out of her chair and helped Tank sit up. She plumped and straightened his pillows.

"I brought you something," said Zach. "It's an electronic game. You can play it by yourself or with someone else. Want to see how it works?"

"Gosh," said Tank. "Thanks. Ya didn't have ta do that. Maybe I'll play it later with my dad if he comes by. I'm kinda tired right now. All I ever do is sleep."

"That's prob'ly good," said Zach. "You'll be good for any visitors that way. What's with all the TV cameras and stuff in here, Tank?"

"Mom says the nurses can keep a better eye on me during the night."

"That makes sense. Guess I should go, Tank," said Zach. "Don't want to wear you out. I'm glad I got to see you. I'll tell everybody you're doin' okay. Take it easy. Maybe I'll come back tomorrow. Can I Mom? If it's okay with Mrs. Tankarian?"

"I'd like that," said Tank. "We can play this game tomorrow maybe."

"Deal! See ya, Tank." Zach ran out of the room. *He's gonna be all right! Can't wait to tell the guys*. His enthusiasm turned into skipping as he sailed out the door and bumped into a young volunteer who had turned the corner at the same time.

"Whoa! Sorry! Hey, balloons and flowers. Cool. Wonder who those are from?" said Zach.

The girl in the pink and white apron recovered her balance and straightened the bouquet.

"Well, the little card here says it's from a Mr. Potter. Do you know him?" asked the young lady.

"Yeah. Well, sort of," said Zach. "Not really. He was the guy who helped Tank when he got hit by that car."

"That's awfully nice of Mr. Potter," said Mrs. Brown. "Very thoughtful. Now, Zach?"

"Yeah, Mom?"

"Please, slow down, dear."

"Okay," said Zach, "but I got to call everybody when I get home! This is awesome. Tank's going to be okay!"

Chapter 21
Celebrity Surprise

The school bus arrived Monday morning and brought with it endless conversation about Tank, the accident, the police and everything that went along with Friday's tragedy. It also brought the giant get well card that Rosa had carefully stowed in the baggage compartment of the bus.

"I can't believe how many people got the story wrong," said Spencer. "I hope Mrs. Matthews or Mrs. 'G' will straighten everyone out."

"Yeah," said Alex. "The story's got way out there."

"You boys want to grab this card, or should I take it to class for you?" asked Rosa.

"We'll help 'em carry it, Rosa," said Mia. "It's just kinda awkward, that's all. Carry my back-pack, Ellie?"

"Sure, Mia," said Ellie. "I can carry yours, too if you want, Alex."

Alex looked away. "That's okay. Thanks anyway." *Why'd I say that? You're such a dummy, Alex. Why didn't you let her?* He flung his back-pack over his shoulder. "Let's get this thing to class. Hope Mrs. 'G' is in the room so we can keep it safe."

"Hey! Look at all the people at our door," said Becca. "What's Daddy doing here? And there's Mr. Feldon and Mrs. Matthews, and that policeman. Wonder who else is here?"

"Come on in kids," said Mrs. Gunderson. "Put your card over there, Alex. The class can sign it later. What a fantastic job! I'm sure Tank will *really* appreciate this."

"What's with all the people?" asked Ellie. "And the TV and stuff?"

"You'll see after the bell rings," said Mrs. Gunderson. "I have just enough time to go get the man from the newspaper."

"Newspaper?" asked Spencer. "What gives?"

"Got me," said Mia. "Why do we need a newspaper guy? Think we'll be on TV?"

It didn't take long to get the class into their seats and quiet in spite of all the confusion.

"Good morning class," said Mrs. Gunderson. She introduced all the adults in the room. "Now, before we proceed with all the questions you have about the accident, I have a big surprise for you. Keep your eyes on the TV monitor . . . and . . . in just a minute . . ."

"Hey! It's Tank!" shouted Zach. "It's Tank! He's on TV!"

"That's right," said Mrs. Gunderson. "He can see all of us, too. Good morning, Tank."

"Hey, everybody. This is really cool," said Tank. "So *that's* what all the TV stuff in my room is about."

Tank's mother stood on one side of the hospital bed, and Mr. Potter, now clean- shaven and smartly dressed, was on the other.

"Hi, Tank!" the class yelled back.

"Hey, look," said Alex. "There's Mr. Potter."

"See you got Mr. Potter there with you," said Mia.

"He's been visitin' me every day," said Tank. "He's really nice.

Playin' games with me, too—especially that one you gave me, Zach. I'm startin' to feel better.

Mr. Potter used to be a medic in some old war. That's why he knew how to fix me up."

"That is sooo cool," said Ellie. "Where's your dad?"

"Uh . . . he had to leave," said Tank. "Right now, I'm just glad to see you guys."

"Tank?" said Mrs. Gunderson. "I know you have to be in the hospital for the rest of this week, but we plan to have you with us in class through this TV arrangement. Your mom will pick up the work, and you can keep up with us. How's that?"

"Awesome," said Tank.

"Right now," said Mrs. Gunderson, "I think Spencer, Alex, Zach, and the girls have something to share with you."

Alex pulled out the gigantic card with the help of the others.

"Geez," said Tank. "What's that?"

"It's a get well card," said Alex. "From all of us. Everybody."

"We're gonna have the whole class sign it, and Spence's dad's gonna bring it to you," said Mia.

"Wow! Think he can bring me a Twinkie, too?" asked Tank.

"Maybe. If the hospital will let you have 'em," said Becca, "*and* if it's okay with your mom." She pushed her glasses into place. "We'll send you some."

Mrs. Tankarian nodded. "I think that will be just fine."

The excitement died down, and Mrs. Gunderson, invited the adults in the room to discuss Tank's accident and answer any questions the students had. Everyone finally left except for the newspaper man.

"Now then," said Mrs. Gunderson, "now that that's over, let's begin again, and work through our lessons for today. Still with us, Tank?"

"Yeah, but I'm gettin' kind of tired," said Tank.

"Get some rest then, and join us when you can," said Mrs. Gunderson. "We'll check in on you later."

"Got it," said Tank. He yawned and closed his eyes. The TV went blank.

Throughout the morning, the newspaper man had taken several pictures, listened to the discussion, and scribbled many notes on a small tablet. He tucked the tablet into his pocket and picked up his camera bag.

As he was leaving he said, "Check the newspaper tomorrow, kids. You can read about Tank and your class. Should be some pictures, too. Hope you've all learned a valuable lesson. Goodbye, Mrs. Gunderson. Thanks for inviting me in."

"'Bye," everyone yelled and waved to the newspaper man.

"I'll be sure to get plenty of newspapers tomorrow," said Mrs. Gunderson. "We can read all about our eventful morning. Now, class? Back to work."

Chapter 22
Making Progress

A long two weeks behind him, Tank returned to school with his new wheels.

"Now don't do anything foolish," said Dr. Beegle. "This leg needs time to mend properly. Okay, Tank? And, you had a pretty bad bump on the head, so be careful. Got it?"

"Promise, Dr. Beegle. I'll be careful," said Tank.

Dr. Beegle restricted Tank to a wheel chair until his leg healed and grew strong enough for him to rely on crutches. Spencer and Zach took turns being Tank's drivers. Alex was the lookout for students or teachers who accidentally stepped in their way as they careened around corners and down hallways. More than once, Principal Matthews had given the boys a ticket for speeding or reckless driving.

"Geez, Spence!" yelled Tank, squeezing the arms of the wheelchair. "Watch it, Zach! You guys almost ran over Ellie."

"Hey, you knuckleheads. Slow down!" Ellie jumped out of the way and dropped the clip board she was carrying. *Idiots! What's with guys and wheels anyway?*

"Zach, I ain't lookin' to have another concussion," said Tank. "And, you're supposed to signal, Alex."

"I did. I did," said Alex. "Ellie was walking too slow. Sorry, Ellie." *She looks mighty fine today. Hello? Ellie? See me?* Alex's heart was pounding, but he couldn't bring himself to utter a word.

"You guys are going to be in big trouble if you do that again," said Ellie. She picked up the clip board and smoothed the wrinkles in the paper.

"Feeling better, Tank?" She smiled at him. *He IS kind of cute. Maybe.*

"I'm gettin' there, thanks. Whatcha got, Ellie?" asked Tank.

"It's for the talent show this winter. It's a ways off I know, but Student Council needs a list of everybody who wants to be in it. You guys interested? I'll sign you up."

"Maybe," said Spencer. He looked at everyone. "We got to talk it over first."

"Okay," said Ellie, "but don't wait too long. The list is getting big. See ya. And for heaven's sake, drive better." Ellie walked toward the picnic tables where Becca and Mia were finishing lunch. She turned around and waved at the boys.

"Okay you guys. She's right. S-L-O-W down," said Tank. "I gotta see Dr. Beegle today, and she'll be mighty mad if I come in all banged up and bruised." *Geez. Did Ellie smile at me?*

"We are being careful," said Spencer. "You'll be out of this chariot pretty soon anyway. Mr. Potter taking you home?"

"Yeah," said Tank. "He's kinda been like a grampa to me. It's really cool. He might even come to my soccer games if I ever play again."

"Sure is nice of him to bring you to school every day. What ever happened with your dad?" asked Alex.

"He's not gonna be around much. Least ways not for awhile," said Tank. "Just saw him that day at the hospital. He got caught robbin' a bank with some guys a long time ago. Now he's out of jail, and he don't want to stick around here."

"Too bad," said Spencer. "No wonder you said he maybe died."

"It kind of sucks," said Tank. "He said he'd call me sometime. Maybe he will. Maybe he won't. I never *really* knew him anyways. Mom's okay with it, too. Don't think she really wanted him around."

"Well," said Zach, "at least you got Old Man Potter now. Think he'll be around for our talent show?"

"Maybe," said Tank.

"Got any ideas what we should do for the show?" asked Alex. "You still want to be in it?"

"Why not?" said Zach. "What do we got to lose?"

"How 'bout we do a magic act of some kind? Hats, rabbits, cards? Stuff like that?" said Spencer.

"Okay, genius," said Alex. "What kind of magic do *you* do?"

"Well, I have an idea," said Spencer. "Listen up." The boys put their heads together, and Spencer shared his plan.

"Okay," said Zach. "Something disappears and reappears. How we going to do that?"

"I got some ideas," said Spencer. "You guys can think of something too, you know, if you don't like my idea."

"This could really be great," said Tank. "Bet Mr. Potter'll help. But where we gonna get the money for all the stuff we need?"

"No problem," said Alex. "I have to take care of Mrs. Anderson's animals and water her garden this weekend. Said she'd pay me twenty dollars if I do a good job. I'll save it, and we can add more money if we need it."

"I got some allowance money," said Zach.

"Me too," said Spencer. "But we proba'ly don't need a whole lot with all the stuff Potter has. Bet he's got a lot of things laying around we could use."

"Right," said Tank. "Want me to invite him over so we can tell him our idea?"

"Can't hurt," said Spencer. "Maybe later we could help him clean up his place, too. Like a thanks-for-helpin'-us kind of thing."

"Good idea. I'll ask him when he picks me up after school," said Tank. "Six thirty okay? His name is Dennis—Major Dennis Potter—his war name. Kind of cool, huh?"

"There goes the bell, guys. Let's get back to class," said Alex. "We can sign up for the talent show when we see Ellie. Hope we're not too late." *Think she'd notice how nice I was to her. Maybe she's just too stuck-up. Or maybe she likes Tank now. She can be so lame.*

Chapter 23
Weekend Job

"Okay, Mrs. Anderson." Alex had the phone on 'speaker' so he could write and so Spencer and Zach could listen.

"I wrote it all down, Mrs. Anderson. See if I got it right. Peety Parakeet and Sebastian, your fish, get fed once a day. I change the water for Peety *every* day. Careful she doesn't get out of her cage. Kitty-Kat, gets her box cleaned, but don't let her outside. Bear *can* go out for a little while to run around, and Bear and Kitty-Kat get fed twice a day. Is that right?"

"That's absolutely correct, Alex," said Mrs. Anderson. *"Bear loves to play fetch. Gives him a little exercise, too. Big as he is, he needs it! So you can do that if you want. I'll leave a number here by the phone if you have an emergency. Start tomorrow morning, early if you would. The key will be under the door mat. I'll be back late Sunday evening. Come by Monday after school, and I'll pay you. You might think about watering my garden, too. Any questions?"*

"No, Ma'am," said Alex, "I think I got it."

"And, Alex? Don't be alarmed if things seem a little strange or different in the house. There's been some unusual activity occasionally," said Mrs. Anderson.

"Uh . . . what do you mean?" Alex tried to hide his concern.

"Every once in awhile, things in the house go missing and show up again in odd places. I haven't been able to figure it out yet. But don't worry your little head over it. It's probably just my mind playing tricks on me," said Mrs. Anderson. *"Not to worry."*

"Okay, Mrs. Anderson," said Alex. "I'll take good care of everything. Have a nice trip. 'Bye." He hung up the phone.

"Whoa!" cried Alex. "What if the house is haunted? I don't want to go in there by myself. Anyone want to help me take care of Mrs. Anderson's house and stuff?"

"Ah, she's just getting old," said Spencer. "She prob'ly forgets where she puts stuff. Don't worry. I'll come with you."

"Gee, thanks, Spence," said Alex. "Might be nothing, but it sure sounds spooky. Makes me kind of nervous actually."

"Boy, I'm glad that let's me out!" said Zach. "I ain't interested in finding any old ghosts—not that I believe in 'em or nothin'. I'll just keep workin' with Tank. See what we can do to start our project. Call if anything *UN*-usual happens. Tank and me'll be right over with our super ghost eliminators!"

"You mean Ghost Busters?" Spencer laughed.

"Yeah, whatever," said Zach. "You know what I mean."

"You want to stay over, Spence?" Alex, half pleaded. "That way we can start checking the animals tomorrow morning—together."

"Why not? I'm sure it'll be okay with my folks, but I got to get home first. Be back in awhile. See ya."

"Me too, Alex," said Zach, "but I'll be around. I'm headin' over to Tank's."

"Geez, that's scary," said Tank when he heard about the Anderson house. "Glad I'm not takin' care of it. Gives me the creeps." His legs were still wobbly from lack of exercise, but he managed to drag out the boxes Mr. Potter brought over.

"Looks like you're doing pretty good, Tank," said Zach.

"Yeah, Dr. Beegle thinks so. She's been workin' me pretty hard in therapy. I'll be walkin' good soon."

Zach helped Tank set the boxes on the floor. "So how does this stuff work? Just looks like a bunch of old boxes to me."

"We'll need to clean 'em and paint 'em, but watch this," said Tank. He sat down. "See how each one fits inside the other? One, two, three . . . from big, and smaller, to little?"

"And? What's so big about that?" Zach wanted a better explanation.

"Look. The bottom slides out in each one, and whatever's in it, drops in the next box, like so," said Tank.

"I don't get it," said Zach.

"It's like this," said Tank. "We show the audience all the boxes, empty of course. Then, we put one on top of the other."

"Big deal." Zach was unimpressed. "Then what?"

"We show the audience we're puttin' something in the little box and makin' it end up in the next one and the next one," said Tank.

"So what's going in the box?" said Zach.

"We're hopin' Amy'll let us use her guinea pig," said Tank.

"Right. That's gonna be our first mistake," said Zach. "Remember the last time she *helped* us? It was a major disaster. Besides, she'll prob'ly want to get paid or somethin'. I wouldn't count on it."

"We'll get somethin' to put in the boxes for the show. Don't worry," said Tank. "But that's how they work."

"I guess it's okay," said Zach. "Seems kind of lame. Has Spencer seen this yet?"

"Nah. I sort of told him about it, but he ain't actually seen it." said Tank. "He thinks it'll work. We can plan the whole magic act when him and Alex get done at Mrs. Anderson's fightin' off the ghosts! We got lots of time anyways." Tank laughed. "Wanna help me paint the boxes?"

Chapter 24
Here Goes Nothing

Early Saturday morning, Alex and Spencer biked over to Mrs. Anderson's house. Alex was hesitant now that he took the job and heard about the strange things that were happening.

"Ready, Spence?"

"Ready as I guess I'll ever be," said Spencer. "Come on, Alex. Open the door."

"Key's under the mat just like she said." He opened the door and heard the dog bark. "Hey, Bear! It's me, Alex. Come here, boy."

The retriever's nails clicked and clacked on the hardwood floor as he bounded around the corner. When he saw Alex and Spencer, his tail wagged in grand welcoming sweeps. He ran to the back door, and danced in circles. "Bet he wants out," said Alex.

"You got that right," said Spencer.

"Okay, fella. Out you go!" Alex held the door open. "That's one down. Now where's Kitty-Kat?"

"Call her," said Spencer. "She's probably hiding somewhere. Cats do that you know."

"Here cat. Here Kitty-Kat," Alex called. But no cat came

running. He called again. "Hey, cat! Where are you?" Still no response. "Is this what Mrs. Anderson means by 'things go missing'?"

"Ya don't call a cat *that* way, stupid. It's: here kittykittykitty. Like it's all one word. I'll keep calling. You take care of Peety and Sebastian. How long does Bear get to stay out anyway?"

"Long enough to take care of business," said Alex. "That's all I know. We can play fetch with him after he eats if you want. Think I should water today?"

"One thing at a time, Man. You got to feed these animals and find the cat first. We should prob'ly look the house over real good, too, ya know. Just in case something's different when we come back this afternoon."

"Right," said Alex. He wasn't sure there'd be an afternoon.

Alex took three cans of food from the pantry, one for Kitty-Kat and two for the big Golden Retriever. When he heard the whir of the electric can opener, Bear dashed into the house. His long pink tongue lolled out the side of his mouth, and Alex swore he was smiling.

"Good boy," said Alex. "Just hold your horses, pal. Sit. Here's food fit for a king." *Ugh. This stuff stinks.* He set the dog dish down on the floor and took care of Peety and Sebastian.

"Okay, Spence. I'm ready to check the house. Maybe we'll find the cat, too, since your 'kittykittykitty' call got us a big nothin'."

Alex and Spencer took mental notes as they scouted the house.

"Everything seems like it's okay," said Alex. "No sign of Kitty-Kat. Maybe she'll come out by the time we get back this afternoon. Guess I should put her food out too—on the counter though—away from Bear. He'd eat the dish if he could. If the food's gone by the time we come back, we'll know she's here somewhere."

Bear licked his bowl so hard it slid across the floor and bumped into the wall. "You must have been really hungry, Bear. You lick any harder, the design's going to disappear right off your bowl," said Alex.

Bear looked up. His tongue slapped side to side around his big floppy muzzle cleaning up every last morsel. He wagged his tail, lumbered over to a large pillow, turned a tight circle and dropped. Breakfast over—time for a morning nap.

"See ya later, Bear. Keep an eye out for Kitty-Kat." Alex slipped the house key into his pocket and shut the door. "Think we should worry about Kitty-Kat?"

"Nah," said Spencer. "She'll show. No need to panic—yet. Did seem kind of strange in the guest bedroom though." He picked up his bike.

"What do ya mean?" asked Alex, picking up his own bicycle.

"Remember? Two watches on the dresser. Why would there be *two* watches in the extra bedroom? Mrs. Anderson lives by herself. Right?"

"Yer right. That *is* weird," said Alex. "Wonder what it means?"

"Prob'ly nothin'. Let's hope anyway. Maybe she just likes watches and keeps 'em in that room," said Spencer.

"Hope so," said Alex. "Guess we'll find out sooner or later. Anyhow, we gotta get with Tank and Zach so we can start working up a good magic act for the talent show. Tank says Mr. Potter gave him some kind of boxes we could use."

"So let's go!" said Spencer. "We got a lot to think about, and we can tell the guys all about the house predicament, the missing cat and watches and stuff. They might have some ideas."

Chapter 25
Girls, Girls, Girls—Whatcha Gonna Do?

"We still have lots of time to get ready for the talent show, but it kind of makes me mad," said Becca. "Ellie always wants to do her own thing. I thought she'd do something with us."

"You know Ellie," said Mia. "She can be so stuck up sometimes. I thought she'd team up with us for the talent show, too. But no. She's doin' her ballet thing. Swan Dance or somethin' like that."

"It's Swan Lake, Mia," said Becca. "She *is* a pretty good dancer. Prob'ly trying to impress the guys if you ask me. Did you notice how much attention she's been giving Tank lately? All of a sudden she's Miss Nicey-Nice. Gag."

"Nah. I haven't seen anything goin' on," said Mia. "I always thought she liked Spencer, or Alex, or somebody. That's how much I know. She's always been kind of stuck on herself if you ask me. I still like her, though. Ellie's just too hilarious."

"She's been hanging around Tank a lot," said Becca. "Something to do with the accident maybe? Wonder if Alex 'gets it'. He really likes Ellie, and she totally ignores him. At least right now."

"Got me," said Mia. "Who's got time to figure out Ellie's love life? Like I care anyway. She likes everybody sometime or other. I can't keep up with all her crushes and romances."

"Well, that leaves me and you to work on some kind of a routine with our Hula- Hoops," said Becca. "You okay with that? Hoops I mean?"

"Sure, why not?" said Mia. "We're both pretty good hoopsters. We can jump 'em, swing 'em, toss 'em, and twirl 'em. Should be easy to figure somethin' out. *When* you gonna get those glasses fixed, Becca? With them hangin' off your face like that, you can't concentrate on hoops. They'll go flyin' off your face first time you twirl."

"Duh, Mia. I get it. I got an appointment next week. Maybe I'll just take them off for the show anyway. Meantime, be thinking of some real good music to go with our routine. Something with lots of crazy rhythm, but smooth. And, we don't want to look stupid. Especially if Ellie is going to be all dressed up in her fancy tutu and ballet slippers. We should wear something flashy and sparkly. Makeup even. Okay?"

"Okay, if I have to," said Mia. "Guess I can wear makeup and stuff for the talent show. I've already got some ideas. We'll have a super act."

"Good," said Becca. "We can practice in the social hall at church. I'm sure Dad won't mind as long as nothing's going on. We'll have lots of room to move around. There's even a super sound system."

"Cool," said Mia. "We'll be great! Know what the guys are doin'?"

"Not really," said Becca. "Something about a magic trick I think."

"Anything they do will prob'ly go wrong," said Mia. "Just wait. Bet it's a disaster."

"Mia, for heaven's sake," said Becca, "don't be so negative. It could be puh-fect-ly wun-duh-ful, dah-ling. Maybe they'll *all* disappear." They both laughed at the possibility.

"Let's see if Mom can take us to the thrift store," said Becca. "We can look for something to wear. And, I think we should have four Hula-Hoops—two each. Then we really need to start practicing."

"I got a couple of old hoops. How 'bout tomorrow?" asked Mia. "Can't be soon enough for me."

"Okay," said Becca, "so let's go shopping. And puh-leeze, don't let on what we're doing to anyone. If the boys find out, they'll just make a big joke out of it."

"They make a joke out of everything we do anyway," said Mia. "Like this is any different? Big deal if they find out. We'll be awesome."

Chapter 26
Bear and Kitty-Kat, Round 2

After a long discussion about the kind of magic act the boys would do, Alex and Spencer left Tank's house and biked back to Mrs. Anderson's for Bear and Kitty-Kat's afternoon visit.

"What'd you think of Tank's box idea for the talent show, Spence?" asked Alex. "I think it'll be really okay."

"Yeah," said Spencer. "I think we came up with something awesome. We just need a bunch of practicing to pull it off, and I have to get Amy to let us use her guinea pig."

"Think she'll let us?" asked Alex.

"For a price, of course," said Spencer. "Maybe we'll have to let her introduce our act or something. She might go for it."

"What kind of dumb plan is that?" asked Alex. "She'll say anything. Embarrassing stuff. About us prob'ly."

"That's a chance we'll have to take. With Amy, who knows? I'll work on it," said Spencer. "Just give me time."

"I hope it's better than the last time she *helped*," said Alex. "She really messed things up. Anyway, let's get back to check on Bear and Kitty-Kat. Maybe we'll find her this time. How can a cat just disappear?"

The boys reached the Anderson house, dropped their bikes on the lawn, and ran to the front door. Bear was barking like he was ready to attack anyone standing on the other side.

"Hey, Bear! It's me and Spence!" yelled Alex. "We're comin' in."

Alex unlocked and opened the front door and tucked the key in his pocket. Barking changed to tail-wagging and face-licking as the boys came in and shut the door behind them.

"Out back you go, boy," said Alex. "Me and Spence are going to have another look around the house first. Then we can play ball, okay?"

"Alex, you're talking to a d-o-g," whispered Spencer. "He doesn't understand a word you're saying."

"Wanna bet?" said Alex. "Just wait. Dogs are super smart. You'll see. Now let's check this house again. See what's going on."

"Alex? Didn't you leave food out for Kitty-Kat?" asked Spencer. "Look. Her bowl is empty. Means she's somewhere around here after all."

"Or something else ate her food," said Alex. "Wasn't Bear, though. He's not going to get up on the counter big as he is."

"This is just too weird," said Spencer. He called the cat several more times, but there was no response. "Now what?"

"Let's check through the house again and see if everything's okay," said Alex. "Then we can play fetch with Bear. Maybe we'll find Kitty-Kat this time. I just wish I didn't feel so spooked."

"Least we got Bear here to protect us. I think he'd tear anyone apart if we yelled. Lead the way," said Spencer. "I'm right behind you."

The boys found nothing amiss in the house until they checked the spare bedroom.

"Wow!" said Alex. "You think this room is haunted? Now the watches are gone! There's *nothing* on the dresser. Is *this* what Mrs. Anderson means by '*things go missing*'?"

"Got me," said Spencer. "This is creepin' me out. You scared?"

"I sure ain't comfortable," said Alex. "Nothin's jumping out at us though. That's a good sign. Right? Let's get out of here. Close the door, too. Maybe that's the key, closing the door."

"No problem. Hurry up, Alex! Let's get out of here. We can play a little ball with Bear and go home," said Spencer. "I don't like this."

"Got ya," said Alex. "Weird though."

"What?"

"Doesn't seem like Bear's upset when we check on him. He's not nervous or jumpy or nothin'." "Maybe he's just used to this stuff," said Spencer. "Grab one of his toys, and let's see what kind of a retriever he is."

"Looks like he's already got a ball outside," said Alex. "Come on. Let's give him a run."

The backyard was a large carpet of green surrounded by flowers and shrubs. Bear dug his ball out of the petunias and looked up. His wagging tail invited a game of fetch.

"Hey, Bear! Bring it here, boy."

Bear grabbed the tennis ball in his mouth and trotted over to the boys. "Told you he was smart," said Alex. "Good dog, Bear. Drop the ball. Drop it."

Toss, return. Toss, return. The boys were giving Bear a good workout, Bear loving every minute of his personal attention.

"Okay, Bear," said Spencer. "Last time. We got to feed you guys and go home."

He gave the ball a deep toss toward the garden. Bear slid and rolled. He leaped up and made a mad dash back to the boys.

"Whoa, Bear. Wait! Wait! You stink like a rotten . . . what did you do?" Alex backed up.

"I think it's poop," said Spencer

"What?"

"Poop. You know. Doggy doo-doo. He must of rolled in it."

"Ohhhh, man," wailed Alex. "Now what are we going to do? Bear can't go back in the house this way. We can't leave him outside, and I've had enough of this creepy house."

"We're just going to have to give him a bath," said Spencer. "This stuff needs *lots* of soap and *warm* water or we'll never get it off."

"Oooo-kay," said Alex. "That means in Mrs. Anderson's big tub, by the 'haunted' bedroom. Please tell me you got a better idea."

"I don't think we got any choice," said Spencer. "We gotta do what we gotta do."

Alex and Spencer left Bear outside, took off their shoes and walked down the hall to the large bathroom.

"This is some strange tub, Spencer," said Alex. "I've never seen a tub this big. Glass walls all around it. Even a door. Check out the holes all around the sides, and look at the shape. Who uses a tub shaped like a stop sign?"

"I think it's one of those bubble tubs," said Spencer.

"Bubble tubs?" said Alex. "What's that mean?"

"Well, if it's like my Gramma's, you fill it up, and push a button somewhere and water gushes out those little holes. Think they're called 'jets' or something. We don't have to use the gushing water thing. We can just get in the tub with Bear, scrub him up good and let him shake off, IN-side the tub of course. Then we can dry him off with some towels."

"Okay," said Alex. "Sounds like a plan. Hope we can get him clean. He really stinks."

"Go get him while I get the water going," said Spencer.

"Okay, Spence. I'll be right back with one stinky dog. Hope he likes water."

Chapter 27
How to Give a Dog a Bath

Alex led Bear to the bath tub and coaxed him in. "Thank goodness that wasn't so bad. Hey, he seems to like bein' in the water. So where's the soap?"

"This squeeze bottle looks like soap," said Spencer. "Says, *'Mrs. Benson's Soothing Lavender Mist'* on the label."

"Hand it over," said Alex. "Bear needs to smell like anything but poop. Grab his collar just in case he tries to take off."

In spite of the ruckus, Bear stood calmly in the tub and casually began drinking the bath water. "No, Bear!" yelled Alex. "Don't drink the water. Quick, Spence! Toss me the soap. Let's get this over with. I don't like being so close to that bedroom."

Spencer tossed. Alex grabbed and missed the bottle hurtling toward him. It dropped into the water with a thud and the contents began spilling out. Bear jumped to get out of the way and pulled Spencer head first into the water followed by Alex who was trying to retrieve *'Mrs. Benson's Soothing Lavender Mist'*.

As he floundered for the bottle, his shirt caught on the glass door and pulled it shut. When both boys managed to stand up again,

Spencer still had Bear by the collar, and the bottle was somewhere at the bottom of the tub. At first there was just a little gurgling sound.

"I can't find the bottle!" yelled Alex. "What's that noise?"

"We must of started the water thing, the jets or whatever they're called. Bet one of us hit the ON button when we fell in," said Spencer.

Bear started jumping and turning in circles. Spencer gripped his collar tighter. "Stop, Bear. Hold it! STAY! SIT!"

Spencer finally managed to get Bear to stand still, but the jets pushed the water harder and harder. Mounds of billowing soapy bubbles grew higher and higher.

"Where's the switch?" Alex was panicked.

"It's got to be in here somewhere," said Spencer. "But I can't see anything. The bubbles are getting too deep, and they're climbing up the walls. I can't even see you anymore. Where are you?"

"I'm over here," said Alex. "Tunnel through the bubbles so I can see you."

"I can't. Bear's standing on my foot. How do we get out of here? Where's the door?"

Suddenly, Bear let go with a massive sneeze that sent soapy bubbles exploding everywhere. Spencer let go of his collar. Bear barked and pawed at the door. It opened, and he jumped out carrying a coat of bubbles and soapy water with him. With one mighty shake, the entire bathroom was showered in a million droplets of lavender-smelling soapy water. Bear loped off down the hall toward the kitchen, shaking himself, slip-sliding as he went. The tub turned suddenly silent.

"Found the OFF button!" yelled Spencer.

"Way late," wailed Alex. "Now what are we going to do? Look at me. Look at you! And the floor! LOOK AT THE TUB!"

Great sheets of milky white foam cascaded down the glass walls and filled the octagon tub. The boys stood dripping wet in the knee-deep froth and stared at the trail of bubbles disappearing down the hall.

"Don't panic, Alex," said Spencer. "We can clean this up. After all, it's only water. Grab a towel. We got to corral Bear and get him outside before he gets *everything* else in the house wet."

"Think that's safe?" asked Alex. "What if he gets dirty again?"

"I don't think he'll do anything but shake off and lay in the sun. We just have to chance it," said Spencer. "Too much to do in here right now. Drop your shorts, and take off your shirt, Alex. There's a dryer in the laundry room. At least we can get our clothes dry while we clean up."

Alex hesitated.

"What's your problem, Alex. I've seen you in your underwear before."

"You got to promise not to tell anyone," said Alex. "And don't laugh."

"Tell anyone what? Why?"

Alex dropped his shorts, revealing a pair of red boxers decorated with space ships, rockets, and shooting stars. Spencer tried not to laugh, but he couldn't control the impulse. He doubled over in side-splitting howls.

"I told you not to laugh, Spence. These are my little brother's. All my underwear is in the wash. Mom made me wear 'em."

"Sorry, Alex. That was just way funny. Anyway, we can get our stuff dry here before we have to go home," said Spencer.

"What have I got to lose?" said Alex, "besides my J-O-B, not to mention I've lost Kitty-Kat."

"You're not helping, Alex. Give it up. Kitty-Kat *will* show. I just bet."

Bear found a warm spot on the patio and stretched out while Spencer and Alex mopped up the water with Mrs. Anderson's fancy guest towels. The dryer hummed away, tumbling shirts and shorts. Alex and Spencer went back to the bathroom, picked up the wet towels, and took them to the laundry room. By now the entire house smelled like a field of lavender.

"See if our stuff's dry, Alex," said Spencer. "I feel half naked."

"We ARE half naked, Spencer! And we smell like a bunch of girls. If Mia and those guys get wind of this, we'll never live it down. I know Mom's gonna wonder why I smell like a perfume factory. Think we can wash and dry these towels before Mrs. Anderson gets back tomorrow?"

"We got to try," said Spencer. "Hold on. Let me open the clothes hamper. We can sort the towels later." Spencer lifted the lid.

"Oh, my gosh," said Alex. "Look, Spence!"

There, curled up behind the hamper was Kitty-Kat with five little kittens and two watches. She looked up at the boys and purred. Alex gently dropped the towels into the hamper and Spencer closed the lid. "We can finish this stuff tomorrow morning, Alex. Now that we know the house ain't haunted, we can take our time cleaning up. Let's go tell the guys. And Alex?"

"Yeah?"

"We won't mention your underwear."

"Wise guy." said Alex. "You'll be sorry if you say one word."

Chapter 28
Getting with the Program

September and October proved to be very busy and exciting months for the 'Super Seven'. And, except for the boys getting grounded again in November, fall was uneventful. All along, the fifth-graders had been working on an ambitious goal to raise funds for the outdoor education program.

Becca was elected treasurer. Ellie and Mia did their best to organize projects with the help of other classmates. The money collected from car washes, bake sales, barbeques, and any other activity the students could dream up went to building the outdoor fund.

Finally, January and the long awaited Talent Show was a short week away. The class expected to raise enough money from a spaghetti dinner and the Talent Show to secure their space in the outdoor camp program. Practice and preparation were nearly complete, and the only things left were details.

"Amy, just do it," said Spencer. "We need to use, um . . . we would *like* to use your guinea pig for the talent show, please? He's not going to get hurt or nothin', and he won't *really* disappear."

"Charlie don't want to be in any stupid old show. He's too shy. 'Sides Charlie don't like you."

"Shy? Since when is a guinea pig shy? And what'd I ever do to Charlie?" Spencer's brain was shuffling through ideas. *Come on, come on. This is harder than I thought. She is so dang stubborn.*

"Look, Amy." Spencer was reaching. "You're always dressing Charlie up in doll clothes. Right? How 'bout you and Charlie dress alike and announce our act? That'd be cool, dontcha think? Then you could hand him to me all dressed like a movie star or your favorite singer. You could be our assistant kind of. How 'bout that?" *Sister dear, sometimes I'd like to flush you down the toilet.* Spencer couldn't resist the thought.

"You got any more dimes for me?" asked Amy. "I could do it for more dimes if you got 'em maybe. And I wanna sing, too. That's *my* talent you know."

The argument went on. Finally, Spencer promised that Amy could *sing* the introduction to the boys' act, and he promised that she'd get ten more dimes for her piggy bank. *Won't be long and she'll want quarters and I'll be broke!*

"Okay, Amy, here's the deal. The guys have to agree to your song. We got to hear what you're gonna sing. If we don't like it, you're toast. We'll get some other animal for our magic trick, and you get NO nickels, NO dimes and NO singing. Got it?"

"Sure, Spencey."

"Don't call me Spencey, Amy, or I'll call everything off right now. No money ever again!" *That was stupid! I can't keep that promise.*

"Okay," said Amy. "You guys can use Charlie, but you better be nice to him. I had him a party with all his piggy friends at Thanksgiving, and he was very, very happy."

"Cross my heart, Amy," said Spencer. "We'll be real careful.

Charlie won't get hurt. Now, go find something to wear for you and him, and practice your song, or whatever you're doing. No changin' your mind now. Okay? We've only got another week to practice."

"Okay. So when do I get my dimes?"

Oh, man! Will she EVER quit?

Spencer raced to the kitchen and called Tank. "Everything is set, Tank. Amy's gonna let us use Charlie after all. Guess we can practice with a tennis ball or something, because she won't let Charlie out of her sight until the talent show."

"Geez, Spence," said Tank. "Sounds like that took a lot of work. How'd ya do it?"

"More bribery. More money and stuff, but she finally gave in. We got to let her sing though."

"Sing?" said Tank. "What's she gonna sing."

"Heck if I know," said Spencer. "She won't let us use Charlie if we don't let her sing."

"Hope you know what your doin' Spence," said Tank. "This could be another Amy disaster."

"That's a definite maybe. If you get a better idea, let me know. Anyways, I'll see you guys later."

Chapter 29
Talent Show—Ellie Takes the Floor

The big night finally arrived. Talent show participants were dressed in costumes. People were in their seats. The houselights dimmed and the spotlights focused on center stage.

"Good evening everyone," said Principal Matthews. "Thank you all for coming. It's so nice to see parents and family members here in support of these youngsters. Sit back now and enjoy the show. Your master of ceremonies this evening is our very own fifth-grade teacher, Mrs. Gunderson. Please welcome her to the stage."

The audience applauded.

"Thank you, everyone. Now let me begin by introducing our first act." Mrs. Gunderson ran through the collection of various acts: piano players, singers, jump-ropers, acrobats, and jugglers. Finally, it was time for the 'Super Seven' to take the stage. Ellie's turn came first. She took a big breath, smoothed the feathers on her hat, and adjusted her costume.

"Ladies and gentlemen, please welcome the lovely and talented Miss Ellie Covington, dancing to Tchaikovsky's Swan Lake."

Ellie glided out onto the stage, head high, toes pointing outward to the right and left as she walked. She held one arm arched over her head, the other out to her side. A feather headband rested on upswept hair. Other feathers adorned her white tutu. She stopped center stage, one foot toward the audience; the other foot poised 'on toe' and waited for the music to begin.

"She kinda walks like a penguin with her feet all stuck out sideways like that," whispered Zach. He and the rest of the group were backstage watching.

"Shut up, Zach. That's how you're supposed to walk. Kind of like a duck when you do ballet." Mia's comments were no nonsense and to the point.

"She really *does* know what she's doing, you guys," said Becca. "Now be quiet and watch. Quit fiddling with Charlie, Amy. Your act is coming up next. What you been feeding him anyway? He's gettin' kind of chunky."

"He likes to eat. Charlie wants to watch, too. He told me so. 'Sides, I'm fixin' his costume 'cuz he's very nervous and jumpy."

"I think Ellie looks like a bird," said Tank. *A really beautiful bird.*

"Duh, Tank," said Spencer. "Swan? As in bird? *Swan* Lake? She's *supposed* to look like a bird."

"Still think she looks pretty nice," said Tank.

The music began and Ellie started her pirouettes, and on toe points and dips. She twirled, arms outstretched, and her eyes spotted the same mark every time she turned.

Didn't know she could do stuff like that. Tank was completely mesmerized. *That's so cool.*

Spencer waved his hand in front of Tank's eyes and whispered. "Earth to Tank. Hello? Where are you, Tank?" But Tank just stared straight ahead and concentrated on the elegant swan.

Ellie reached the far side of the stage, made another turn and was about to come back to center when Amy dashed across the stage chasing Charlie.

"Catch him!" she yelled. "Don't let him get away!" The audience gasped.

Charlie, dressed in a little red cape, skittered around behind Ellie's legs followed by Amy, who was also wearing her *magic* red cape.

Before she completed her next turn, Ellie's legs tangled with Amy's cape. Her ankle turned, and they both fell in a heap. Charlie escaped off stage. Tank grabbed him, and stared at the two girls on the floor.

"Here, Spence. Hold Charlie. I got to help Ellie."

"Tank! What's the big deal? She *can* get up by herself you know." *There he goes again! His brain's turned to mush. Think he likes Ellie? Impossible. She can't stand him. What gives?*

Tank reached the middle of the stage and offered his hand to Ellie. She took it, and he lifted her to her feet. His arm slipped easily around her waist as he helped her hop off stage. Tank caught a whiff of her hair. *Geez, she smells nice too.*

The audience cheered. Mrs. Matthews ran onto the stage. "Slight delay, folks. Everything's under control. We'll be back in a minute."

"Ow! Ow! I think I sprained my ankle, Tank. Not so fast." Tears welled up in Ellie's eyes. Now I can't finish my dance, and I worked so hard. This stinks." *Tank? He ran out to rescue me?*

"Thank you, Tank," said Ellie. She sat down in a chair. "I didn't realize you were so strong."

"Wasn't nothin', Ellie. I know what it feels like to get hurt. Just tryin' to help."

Never seen her so helpless like, and cryin'.

"You okay, Ellie?" Mia knelt down and examined her ankle. "Becca's gettin' some ice with Mrs. Matthews, and your mom's comin' up. Just sit still 'til she gets here. I got to help Amy with Charlie. He's really a squirmy worm for some reason. Prob'ly too much going on for him."

"I'll be okay, Mia." *Thanks to Tank.* "Go do what you have to. Why did Amy let go of that stupid little rodent anyway? She completely ruined my dance. She's always ruining everything!" *She wouldn't last ten minutes if she was my sister.*

Mia found Amy and helped her calm Charlie down. They straightened out his cape and adjusted the little black hat that was secured under his chin. "I don't think he likes this, Amy. Maybe you should take it off."

"No way! Me and him are dressed alike just like Spence said we should. I'll take it off when we're done, but first, we got to pa'form. We're next ya know. And, I get to pronounce the act after I sing."

"Whatever, Amy. Knock yourself out. Break an arm, or leg, or however that goes." Mia had enough fooling around with Amy.

Amy tucked Charlie under her chin and sang her song to him. "Be quiet now, Charlie. It's gonna be our turn in one minute."

Chapter 30
The Boys Take Center Stage

The Talent Show resumed after the Ellie/Charlie escapade into somewhat of a normal routine. "And now for your enjoyment," began Mrs. Gunderson, "here are the Fantastic Four Magicians, introduced by Miss Amy Johnson."

Amy skipped out to center stage holding Charlie, and her magic wand. She straightened her cape and hat, and blinked at the spot light. "Bright," she said. "This is my song for Spency. He's my brother you know. And for Tank, Zach and Alex. They're just boys. Thank you." She curtsied. "Quiet, Charlie." She whispered to the little wiggly rodent.

"What the heck is she doing, Spence?" Alex whispered. Tank and Zach just shook their heads.

"This ought to be good," said Mia.

Twinkle, twinkle little staaaaaar,

Amy's voice wavered up and down as she sang out the familiar tune. Spencer just glared at her.

These four boys will take a caaaar,
They have a trick for you to seeeee,

Then they're s'posed to eat a treeee,
After they hide my pet Charlieeee. She bowed.

The audience laughed, applauded and waited for whatever was to follow from the Fantastic Four. "Move it *Spency*." Zach mimicked Amy.

"Don't call me that again, Zach, or I'll punch you right here."

The boys walked out dressed in their magician attire. Tank spotted Mr. Potter in the audience with his mother and he waved. *Geez! He came. Cool. Camera too.* Mr. Potter gave a 'thumbs up'.

Each of the boys carried one of the boxes, except for Spencer. He took Charlie from Amy and leaned in close to her. "Your stupid song didn't make any sense, Amy. That's not what you said you were going to sing, and I told you NOT to call me Spency." *How do I live this down? Now everyone's going to call me Spency. You're fried, you little twerp.*

Mysterious music played from the loud speakers, the lights dimmed, and the boys began their act. Tank held the largest box, Zach took the middle-sized one, and Alex held up the smallest box. Amy removed her cape. It became the 'magic cloth' for the show.

"Think anything'll go wrong?" Mia whispered to no one in particular. The girls watched intently. Ellie had her ice-wrapped foot propped up on a chair.

"Who knows," said Becca. "With these guys and Amy, anything's possible. Just watch."

Amy pointed to each box with her magic wand as the boys showed the audience they were empty. "And now, we will stack them together, put Amy's guinea pig, Charlie, inside the small box and make him reappear in the second box." Tank spoke in a firm announcer-like voice. He set the boxes on a low table. Spencer removed the little hat and cape from Charlie. "Put him in Spence. Get him in here," whispered Tank.

Charlie kept wiggling, but once Alex threw the magic cloth over the box, he quieted down. Amy waved her wand over the box. Tank slid the hidden gate and Charlie dropped into the second box.

Amy yanked the cloth away. Alex picked up the small box and showed the audience. "Empty!" he said. The audience cheered. "Charlie is now in the second box." He tipped the box for the audience to see. "Now he will magically appear in the third box." Alex set the small box down and stepped back for Zach's turn.

Once again, the cloth was placed over the second box. Amy repeated the wand waving, and Tank tried to slide the second gate for a few minutes. This time, the gate was more difficult to move. *What the? Settle down, Charlie.* Finally, Amy yanked the cloth away, and Zach showed the empty box to the audience, again followed by wild cheers and murmurs.

Amy was about to throw the magic cloth over the third box when Tank held up his hand and stopped her. "Geez, you guys. Look!" he whispered. The audience waited for the hold-up. Amy grabbed the first look and screamed.

"You guys chopped Charlie into little pieces!" she screamed. "I said you could not hurt him! You killed Charlie!" She ran off stage crying to Mrs. Gunderson. People in the audience began to mumble. *What happened? Don't know. Think they killed him?*

"Geez, Amy. Hold on!" Tank yelled across the stage. "Charlie's fine. Come here and look." Tank set the box down. Amy and the guys examined it. Tank looked out at the audience. "Seems like Charlie is more of a Carlie. He . . . um, she just had a little baby." *No wonder I couldn't slide the gate.*

Amy dried her eyes and walked back to the box. "That was a

very good trick, Spency. How'd ya do it? How'd ya change Charlie into two piggies?"

"We didn't do nothin', Amy. I think Charlie's party did it," said Tank.

"Ya mean when his friends came over at Thanksgiving?" She was confused.

"Prob'ly," said Spencer. "Some friend got too friendly. We'll talk later. Take a bow."

The crowd clapped and cheered. Tank carried the box off stage. Amy held onto it with one hand.

"Put it down, Tank! Put it down! I wanna see," said Amy.

Tank set the box down in front of Ellie so she could see too. "Ain't that somethin'? A little pup. Bet she'll have more before the show's over. Ya need to put some paper in the box Amy, and keep an eye on her. How's your foot, Ellie?"

"Could be better, thanks. The ice helps."

"Mind if I sit by ya? I got to see what Mia and Becca's gonna to do."

"Sure, Tank." She looked up at him. *He seems taller. Thinner?* "Have a seat." She patted the chair next to her.

"Thanks." *She's bein' dang nice to me for a change. Girls. Go figure.*

Mia and Becca gathered up the Hula-Hoops, moved close to the curtains and waited for their cue to go on.

"How we goin' to top that one, Becca? All we got is a stupid hoop dance."

"Don't worry, Mia. Just do the dance we practiced. We'll be awesome." *I hope.*

Chapter 31
Mia and Becca Turn Up the Action

With the confusion over, the show resumed. "Now for our last act, I'd like to present Mia Matsuzaki and Rebecca Bailey, 'The Sparkling Heart Beats' and their twirling hoops."

A lively foot-tapping song with a swinging beat swept over the audience. Mia and Becca skipped out to center stage, Hula-Hoops in hand. They were dressed alike in pink shirts with a large sparkly heart printed on the front. A rhinestone headband held back their hair. Sparkling hearts were sewn on the back pockets of purple shorts. They glued sparkles on the toes of their shoes, glittered their cheeks, and eye brows. 'Sparkle' fit them perfectly.

They glanced at each other, stepped apart, nodded their heads to the beat of the music, and began their routine. They twirled, jumped, spun and rolled the hoops back and forth to each other.

"They look pretty good," whispered Spencer. *Especially Becca, he thought.* "I couldn't do that stuff." *She's actually kinda cute. Maybe.*

"Yeah, that's cool how they can spin 'em out and make 'em come back." Alex watched the girls with the critical eye of an artist. "You guys notice anything different?"

"What?" they asked.

"About the girls."

"Nah," said Zach. "It's just Mia and Becca with make-up and shiny stuff. What do ya mean?" Zach studied the dancing forms on the stage. "I got nothin'."

"They just look girly. Never seen Mia like that before." Spencer tried to see what Alex saw. "You mean? You mean . . ." He snickered.

"Yeah," Alex whispered. "I think Mia is actually wearin' a bra."

"Shut up!" Spencer choked back the urge to burst out in laughter.

"What are you guys whispering about?" asked Ellie. "Surprised they can do so good?"

"Right. Yeah. You're right, Ellie," said Spencer. "We're just taking in the routine." He elbowed Zach and Alex. *Wouldn't she like to know what we're takin' in!*

The girls were spinning the hoops around their waists and arms and feet. The act was impressive.

Becca stepped back in true showmanship and let Mia take the stage alone to show off her arm/wrist twirling techniques. About the third time around, the spinning hoop slipped off Mia's wrist and went flying out into the audience. It smacked Mr. Feldon, the school counselor, square on the forehead and dangled around his neck like a giant necklace. *Oh my gosh. What have I done? I've knocked out Mr. Feldon. Did I kill him? Shoot.*

Becca lost her concentration, and focused on the commotion around Mr. Feldon. Mia forgot the performance, leapt off the stage and was now at his side. "I'm so sorry, Mr. Feldon. It just got away from me. Are you okay? Are you hurt?"

"I'm okay, Mia." He handed the hoop back to Mia, and rubbed

the red mark emerging on his forehead in the shape of a hot dog. "Go for it, Mia. Go finish your act." But all Mia could do when she reached the stage was grab Becca.

"I think I'm done. Let's just bow and get out of here, okay? I'm so embarrassed. And this bra you loaned me is killin' me. Why'd you make me wear it anyway?"

"Mia, get over it. You *need* it," said Becca.

"Sure, Becca. And who made *you* the boss of my boobs?"

They bowed and walked off stage holding their hoops.

The audience stood and applauded the evening's events. *Bravo! Great! Super!* Everyone came back on stage for a second bow including Ellie who hopped out holding onto Tank's arm. *He IS taller. Kind of cute actually with that curly red hair.*

Spencer stuck a finger in his mouth and pretended to gag. *Tank, you're askin' for it. She's trouble! Get away before it's too late.*

"Tank's got a girlfriend, Tank's got a girlfriend." Amy chimed in.

"Knock it off, Amy. I'm just helpin' her," said Tank. *Wonder if Ellie's just bein' nice 'cuz she's hurt. Or maybe? Nah.* Tank's mind was racing.

The evening ended with hugs and flowers from eager parents who rushed to the stage to congratulate the students. Amy was delighted with her brood of guinea pigs, and except for Ellie's ankle, the Talent Show was a great success. Tank looked around for his mother. She was talking to a friend. He felt a hand on his shoulder and turned around.

"Hey, Mr. Potter. Thanks for comin'. It was nice to see you given us guys 'thumbs-up' for our performance. I think we did good, too."

"You don't have to call me 'Mr. Potter', Tank. It was just really nice for me to be part of a family again. You can call me Dennis, or Grampa Potter if you want."

Tank wrapped his arms around Mr. Potter in a big bear hug. "Geez, thanks Mr. um. . . . Grampa. This is the best day ever!"

Chapter 32
The Countdown

Becca, class treasurer and representative in charge of promoting fundraising for the outdoor education event, took the money box down from the classroom closet. Mrs. Gunderson looked up from her paperwork, smiled and nodded. Becca and the girls sat outside the classroom at the conversation table and calculated the earnings from the talent show.

"So how much did we make?" asked Mia.

"Looks like the barbeque and talent show brought in enough to pay for our bus to Newly Harbor," said Ellie. She and Mia counted the last of the change. "Everyone just has to turn in the rest of their money and in a few weeks, it's Campo del Mar here we come! You guys get sea sick?"

"I don't," said Mia. "Went deep sea fishing with my dad once, and it didn't bother me. What's a del Mar anyway?"

"Means 'of the sea' or 'by the sea', something like that," said Ellie. "Camp by the Sea. We've been out on the ocean in our boat a million times, and I've never been sea sick. How 'bout you, Becca? You get sea sick?"

"No idea," said Becca. "Never been out on the ocean before, but I'll be fine. I would definitely NOT like getting *any* kind of sick. Barfing is so gross."

"Well, it takes about an hour to get to the island, and if the water's nice, shouldn't be a problem. Might even see dolphins on the way over." Ellie spoke like she was a seasoned tour guide. "It ought to be really fun. Of course, now I need to go shopping."

"What a shock," said Mia. "Must mean your ankle has miraculously healed."

"Give it a rest, Mia. Of course my ankle's not healed, but it's good enough to go shopping," said Ellie. "Dr. Beegle said so. Long as I keep it wrapped. Want to come? I need a new swim suit, and pajamas, and tennies and flip-flops. And . . . your very valuable opinions, of course." *I've got to look cool. Just in case somebody notices me.*

"Why don't ya just take Becca? She knows more about clothes than me. Especially about bras. Right Becca?" *I know the guys were making fun of me. Stupid jerks and I don't need to watch you spend money, Ellie.* Mia mentally rehearsed the awful talent show disaster.

"That's mean, Mia. Just because I *encouraged* you to wear a bra for the talent show, doesn't mean I'm a know-it-all," said Becca. "You were just kind of bouncy, that's all. I thought you would look better. More together. Especially after our Health class on 'Middle Grade Maturing' or whatever that thing was called. Some day you'll thank me."

"Wanna bet? That was *the* most embarrassin' Health class I *ever* had," said Mia. "I just wanted to crawl inside my backpack and never come out. I could see the guys starin' at us every time the nurse talked about '*our physical changes*', and '*hormones*', and '*moodiness*'. I never felt so stupid in all my life. Even ringin' Mr. Feldon's neck with my Hula-Hoop wasn't *that* bad."

"The guys prob'ly felt really stupid too," said Ellie. "One time I looked over at Tank and his face was all red. It was so embarrassing. But, hey. That's over Mia, so just drop it. Do you guys think Tank'll get to go to outdoor camp? Is it his grades? I could maybe tutor him."

"Man, you *really* got it bad, Ellie," said Mia. "What's with all this stuff about Tank, Tank, Tank? Thought you couldn't stand him. By the way, he never goes *anywhere* overnight. Haven't you noticed? Says his mom won't let him. So I bet he won't make it, and I really don't care. I don't care if any of 'em go." *Brainless twits. Always showin' off an' actin' big-time.*

"Hello? Becca here. I thought we were talking about shopping? Why don't we all go? I need stuff too, and I promise I won't make you look at any bras, Mia. Bet mom would drop us at the mall. No pressure. We can just look at stuff."

"Okay by me," said Ellie.

"Oh, all right." Mia reluctantly agreed to tag along. "Maybe I'll find some cool sunglasses." *The guys can make fun of those all they want. I don't give a darn.*

Becca took the money box to Mrs. Gunderson and colored in two more spaces on the gigantic paper thermometer tacked to the bulletin board in the classroom: **Campo del Mar Fundraising Goal**. *Almost there! I can hardly wait. Wonder if Spencer got my note?*

Mrs. Gunderson looked up from her paper-grading. "This class is doing a marvelous job at raising money. You girls excited?"

"You bet, Mrs. 'G'. This'll be my first campout, without my parents anyway. I can hardly wait," said Mia with more enthusiasm than necessary. *Just hope I don't get homesick, or sea sick. What'll make me really sick is taking a shower in front of all the other girls. That will be one giant problem.*

The conversation at Spencer's house followed the same outdoor education chatter. Zach, Alex, and Tank hovered around Spencer's video game taking turns squaring off against each other in the virtual football game.

"You guys got everything for the camp-out? I just need a couple more things and I'll be ready to go," said Spencer jerking the controls. "Ha! Gotcha, Zack. Touchdown!"

"Yeah," said Zach, "I'm almost ready, too." He pressed a button on his controls and blocked the runner with the football. "No score, Spence. Didn't ya see the flag?"

"I got everything I need," said Alex. "My brothers got so much stuff to loan me, I don't need anything. Glad you *finally* get to go overnight someplace, Tank."

Alex took the controls from Spencer. "Blocked your kick, Zach. Now what're you gonna do?"

"I ain't gonna miss this for nothin'," said Tank. Once Mr. uh . . . Grampa Potter said he'd come along to chaperone, Mom was okay with it." Tank's mind wandered.

"I know," said Spencer. "That's so cool, Tank. Hope all of us get to bunk together while we're at Camp del something or whatever it's called.

Spencer fiddled with the note in his pocket. *Wonder what Becca means? Study partner. Girls. Who can figure 'em out.* "Anybody got an idea of just a small trick we can play on the girls while we're there?"

"You heard Mrs. 'G', Spence. Anyone gettin' caught doin' nonsense gets sent home. I don't wanna get sent home. 'Specially with Grampa Potter comin' along." Tank showed real signs of concern for once in his life.

"Well maybe we can just have a little fun." Spencer's mind was working.

"Fun's one thing, Spence," said Zach. "You really better think about this one. If somethin' does happen, guess who the teacher will be lookin' for? I don't wanna get sent home. Shoot. Game over. You win, Alex."

"Bet I can come up with something eventually," said Spencer. "Le'me know if you guys get any ideas. We still got time to be creative. How much you wanna bet the girls are thinkin' up somethin', too?"

Chapter 33
Waiting Over

February and March came and went. Mr. Potter enjoyed his new 'Grampa' relationship with Tank, and helped him get ready for the Science Fair and the outdoor education trip.

For the most part, even the Science Fair went smoothly. Amy burst into tears when some kids poked fun at her 'Anatomy of a Guinea Pig' project. They thought her drawings looked more like frogs with ears and short legs.

Spencer and Tank put together the favorite volcano experiment with a twist. "It's been done so many times, boys," said Mrs. Gunderson. "Think of something to make it unique."

"How 'bout we make a moat around the volcano? Sort of like a mountain coming out of a lake," said Tank.

"Cool," said Spencer. "We can make it really awesome."

Trouble was, when they poured vinegar into the top of the volcano, the bubbling 'lava' grew with such unpredictable energy, the mountain exploded, broke open the moat, and a watery mess bubbled over an entire exhibit table ruining the work of four other students. The boys were forced to withdraw their project and help the befuddled students rebuild their entries.

Zach's model car powered by solar energy was extremely popular. Alex's presentation on how the eye translates color in the brain, earned him a First Prize ribbon.

Mia, Becca, and Ellie combined forces to show how music and light affect growing plants. They earned a Second Place in the Botany Division.

Once the Science Fair was over, full concentration turned to the May Outdoor Education Project, now just one week away. Eager fifth-graders were counting down the hours to the three-day campout.

The class had at last reached its goal for going to Campo del Mar. "Finally, boys and girls," said Mrs. Gunderson, "tomorrow morning we're on our way to camp. Be here at school by 5:00 AM. No stragglers! Tell your parent chaperones, too. Rosa has to load our gear on the bus, and we have a boat to catch. Any problems? Call me on my cell phone, otherwise, 5:00 AM sharp—with your packed lunch! Does everyone understand?"

A loud "YES" rose from the group of anxious campers.

"It's a long ride to the harbor, so eat a good breakfast, especially if you've taken any sea-sick medication," said Mrs. Gunderson. "You can buy a snack on the boat if you're hungry, but save your lunch for the island. We'll be hiking in to our camp site, and you'll be mighty hungry by then. Got it?"

"YES!" Again came the unanimous answer.

"Okay, then. I'll see you all bright and early tomorrow morning." Mrs. Gunderson waved everyone out the door, sat down at her desk, and checked her clipboard for last minute details. *Another year, another camp. Lord, please let it all go well!*

Chapter 34
And They're Off!

Noses counted, chaperones strategically placed around the bus for crowd control, and the baggage compartment secured meant at last the fifth-grade class was off to Newly Harbor. Mia, Becca, and Ellie chose a seat near the front of the bus while Spencer, Tank, Alex, and Zach sat in the back. Grampa Potter wasn't far from the four boys.

"So two hours, huh? That's how long it takes to get to the harbor?" asked Zach. "Man, what're we gonna do for *two* whole hours? That's like a lifetime."

"I have my good ol' sketch book," said Alex, "so you know what I'm gonna do."

"How 'bout we play cards?" said Spencer. "That'll take up some time. I brought my headphones, too." He reached into his sweatshirt pocket for the cards and felt the wadded up note he'd kept from Becca. *Study partner. What in the heck does she mean? Maybe I should just dump it.*

"I brought the game ya gave me, Zach. Why don't you and me play that? We can trade off or somethin'," said Tank.

"Later, Tank," said Zach. "Right now I'm gonna listen to music."

"Guys? How much studyin' do you think we'll *really* be doin' at camp?" asked Spencer. "Think we'll have study partners and stuff?"

No one answered. No one wanted to. This was all a new and exciting adventure requiring serious daydreaming, and for awhile, the boys were lost in thoughts of campfires, hiking, snorkeling, and kayaking.

At the front of the bus, Ellie, Mia, and Becca had their heads together discussing the items they brought along for the trip.

"*Another* diary, Ellie?" said Becca. "Don't you ever go anywhere without that thing?"

"I got a new one just for *this* trip, and a camera too. I want to document everything for Student Council," said Ellie with all the professionalism of a news reporter. She opened the diary to show the girls her new journal. On the inside cover, there it was—a small heart with the initials, T T + E C.

"Oh, for cryin' out loud, Ellie. Have you lost your mind?" Mia gagged. "That's 'Tank plus Ellie' I'm guessin'?"

"It's nothing, Mia," said Ellie. "Just playing around with initials. Tank *has* been awful nice to me you know. Especially after I hurt my ankle. He even gave me this pen." She waved it under Mia's nose. "Smells nice, too."

"So I suppose that means you *have* to like him now? Like he's your boyfriend or something?" Mia was amazed at how many times Ellie could change her mind.

"Give it up, Mia. Ellie's *always* got someone on the line. Get back to the checklist," said Becca. She had her own mind focused on Spencer. *He's so cute in a nerdy kind of way. No answer to my note though. Maybe he threw it away.* She was mentally orchestrating ways to get him to work with her at camp.

"Well, I brought something special. Something I bet we can trick the boys with," said Mia.

"We're *not* going to risk doing anything stupid, Mia," said Becca. "I don't want to get sent home just because *you* decided to dream up a dumb get-back. Why can't we just forget it this time?"

"Ha!" said Mia. "You think for one minute those guys aren't dreamin' up somethin' for us?"

"I *hope* not," said Ellie. "I just want to have fun without worrying about those dorks. They'll be in major trouble if they get caught trying anything. Just keep it to yourself, Mia. Besides we *do* have assignments while we're there, you know. So don't mess us up."

"We'll see," said Mia. "We'll see." She pulled a set of ear phones out of her pocket, plugged into a game device, and turned it on.

Becca opened a favorite book while Ellie concentrated on documenting *The First Day of the 5th Grade Trip* by Ellie Covington. For the moment, the girls were quiet.

The bus rumbled south along the freeway toward Newly Harbor. The early hour, lack of coffee, and the droning of the bus engine encouraged several of the chaperones to drift off. Mrs. Gunderson looked around. She smiled her 'thank you smile' silently acknowledging the adults that had agreed to accompany the class. *Better sleep now, people. Heaven knows there won't be much of that for the next three days!*

Chapter 35
Do You See What I See?

The school bus finally pulled into the parking lot at Newly Harbor and there it was. Like a sleek white whale with large blue stripes, the sixty-five foot craft bobbed in its slip, diesel motors humming, waiting for departure. Sunlight glistened in random patterns on rippled water. **Starship II**, the name printed across its stern.

"Man, look at that!" Spencer poked Tank in the ribs so hard he yelped.

"Easy, Spence!" Tank rubbed his side. "Wow. I never been on a boat this big. Check out that open part."

A four foot wide section on the side of the boat opened downward and rested on the dock creating a ramp for passengers and crew to get on board.

"Guess that's where we're s'posed to get on," said Zach, standing up and stretching.

"Don't see any other way," said Alex. "No ladders or nothin'. Let's get off this old bus and give Rosa a hand with our stuff."

"Want any help, Rosa?" Spencer offered, hoping he and the boys could speed up the detail.

"Just sit tight, kids. I have to do this. Insurance and all that. Wouldn't want you to get hurt. But thanks anyway."

The excited group waited with strained patience for Rosa and the chaperones to unload the cargo bay of the bus. "That's it Mrs. Gunderson." Rosa wiped her forehead. "I'll be back to get you in three days. Stay safe, everybody." She turned, waved to the group, and climbed into the bus.

"Okay, kids and chaperones," said Mrs. Gunderson, "pick up your things and follow me."

Mia eased in behind Spencer and the rest of the boys clamoring up the ramp each carrying a variety of personal belongings. She was as anxious to examine the boat as the boys were.

Bags and bundles dropped into a disorganized pile on the floor of the lower deck. Mia watched a small item slip from Spencer's sleeping bag. Before anyone had time to notice, she snatched it up and tucked it into her sweatshirt. *Unbelievable! Wait 'til I show the girls.*

"Let's scope this baby," said Spencer.

"Lead the way, Spence. Wonder what's up there?" said Alex, pointing to the stairs.

The short climb led to the enclosed mid section or 'tween deck. A crew member was making coffee in the galley, the boat's kitchen, and arranging sandwiches and treats for hungry passengers.

"Good morning, fellas. Be a few minutes before I'm ready for customers. Come back a little later."

Tank's eyes were drawn to a tray of Twinkies next to the doughnuts and Danish. A definite return trip to the galley was on Tank's mind.

Tables and booths lined the sides of the boat next to water-spotted Plexiglas windows. Here, passengers could eat, read, play cards, or just keep warm when the boat was moving. Outside, a waist-high wall surrounding the boat's mid section, protected passengers from falling overboard while the craft was moving. Another set of stairs, more like a ladder, led to the upper deck.

"Welcome to the top of the world, boys," said Ellie. She'd been one of the first to claim her 'personal' viewing spot. "I plan to be up here for the whole trip!" She sat cross-legged on one of the benches and fiddled with her camera. "Smile," she said, pretending to snap a picture of the boys. Mia and Becca leaned over the rail and watched the activity below.

"This is really high," said Becca. "Hope the boat doesn't tip over."

"I think we're just fine, Becca," said Mia. "Bet it'll be windy and a little rocky up here—no biggy."

The upper deck had rows of benches, and another walkway enclosed by a three foot high railing, so seemingly unnecessary while the craft wasn't moving. Still higher, like a little cubicle, was where the ship's captain sat to maneuver the boat. The small room was surrounded by windows, gages, radios, lights, horns, large vertical throttles and a steering mechanism. This was the navigation center or bridge. Here, the captain could see 360 degrees to steer the boat, spot running kids, bark orders to the crew, and point out anything of interest in the channel. Reaching even higher were four tall antennae, the radio link to the harbors.

"Who's that dude?" Zach pointed toward the small cabin.

The weathered-looking man in a stocking cap sat at the helm above all the passengers. He stroked an unkempt beard and squinted at the horizon. Flannel sleeves hanging below a faded sweatshirt spoke of many sea-driven days. His mysterious looks told of storms, rocky seas, and adventure.

"My guess is that'd be the guy who drives the boat," said Alex.

"It's not a dude," said Spencer. "He's the captain. He *operates* the boat. He steers it. He doesn't drive it."

There was a loud click and the air was filled with a booming voice.

"*Campers and passengers,*" began the Captain, "*please find a seat and prepare for departure. No running, boys and girls—feet on the ground at all times and don't lean over the rail. We don't want to pull anyone out of the drink!*" He chuckled. "*We should have a pleasant trip, calm seas, maybe spot some marine life. Mind the adults and ask questions. We're here to help you get acquainted with the sea.*" Click.

The engines roared to life and the craft began to move slowly out of the harbor and toward the open sea. Once out of the harbor, the boat picked up speed causing everyone to grab railings or teeter awkwardly against the rhythm of the moving vessel.

"Geez, this is sweet!" said Tank. "I got to find Grampa Potter. Bet he likes this, too. Maybe grab me a Twinkie while I'm at it."

Within minutes **Starship II** was joined by a group of frolicking dolphins who seemed to be playing a game in the forward wake of the fast-moving boat.

"Oh, my gosh. Did you see that?" Zach pointed to the leaping animals. "Look how high they can jump! Man, they're fast!"

Click. "*Ahead of the boat, kids, are dolphins—smallest of the whale family, although some people will argue about that. There are approximately 25,000 of them living in the channel between Newly Harbor and Campo del Mar. They love to chase and play with fast-moving boats.* Click.

"They almost look like they're smiling," said Alex. "Did ya see that? It went right under the boat. Wish I could touch one!"

With hair flying and voices cut by the wind, Zach, Spencer, and Alex parked themselves at the bow where they could watch the nose of the boat slice through the water. They were completely mesmerized and fascinated by the pod of dolphins that raced against the fast moving vessel.

At the crest of the next wave, the boat rode its downside sending sheets of salty spray over the youngsters. "Wow!" yelled Spencer. "Some ride!"

Chapter 36
Off to the Island

With all the abandonment of pirates, the students swayed and jumped with every toss of the boat, screamed in delight when waves crashed over the bow, soaking them, and watched for signs of sea life pointed out by the captain.

Click. *"We're slowing a little, folks,"* said the captain. *"Possibly some whales on the starboard side of the vessel—that's the right side for all you land lubbers."* He chuckled. *"They're migrating now. Keep your eyes open for the whale's giant exhale spray called a 'blow' when it comes up to breathe. Long ago, whalers would shout 'Thar she blows!' if they spotted a whale. Now we just shout 'BLOW!' if we see a spout—but, that's another story. Anyway, when the whale comes up to fill its lungs with air, it dives and leaves a large, flat ring on the surface of the water called a 'footprint'. Keep your eyes open!"* Click.

"I see it! I see it!" yelled Mia. "Look, you guys! There it is!" She grabbed Becca by the arm. Becca stood silent in disbelief that anything could be so big.

About fifty yards out, the huge Gray surfaced, spewing a tower of mist from the blowhole atop its head. It arched its back and slid back into the deep.

Click. *"Last thing you'll see is the whale's dorsal fin or its wide, flat tail—sometimes 25 feet across on the Humpbacks,"* said the captain. *"They're called flukes. Whales can hang out in the deep for quite awhile before coming back to the surface unless it's a female and her calf. Then they don't go so deep."* Click.

Ellie stood straddle-legged, trying to steady herself amidst the jostling passengers and rocking of the boat. She pointed the camera toward the spot where the whale was last seen when she felt some-one step in next to her.

"Need some help, Ellie? I can hold your arm if you like," said Tank.

"Hey," said Ellie. "Thanks, Tank. Just keep me steady for a min-ute while I get a couple of pictures for our Year Book. Like the ride so far?"

"Couldn't be better. 'Specially since Grampa Potter is along. He's tellin' me lots about the ocean and stuff. Sure glad he wanted to come."

"He seems like a really nice person, Tank," said Ellie. "Nice he could be with you. And Tank? I hope you guys aren't planning any-thing stupid while we're at camp."

"It ain't gonna be me if there is," said Tank. "I don't want to get sent home and I sure don't want to 'barrass Grampa Potter."

"Good," said Ellie. "I just want to have fun while we're at camp without worrying about some dumb get-back. Maybe you and I can do a study project or something together. Let me know if you hear anything, if you know what I mean."

"Sure thing, Ellie," said Tank. "See ya."

"Right." Ellie wandered off to find Mia and Becca. The girls were seated in the galley working on a cup of hot chocolate. "Hey!" she shouted. "Where've you been? I've been all over the place looking for you guys. What's up anyways?"

"After the whale and dolphin sighting, we just wanted to get in out of the wind," said Becca.

"I got some great pictures," said Ellie. "Did you guys see that funny looking sun fish? What a trip. I can't figure out how a round fish manages to swim without tipping over. Saw Tank, too. Told him to let us know if the guys were planning anything dumb."

"Big deal," said Mia. "If they do, someone is going to be in for a very big surprise."

"Like what?" asked Ellie. "You know I said no trouble, Mia."

"Well, look what fell out of Spencer's sleeping bag." Mia looked around the galley for familiar faces. Satisfied there were no spies, she reached into her sweatshirt pocket and pulled it out.

"Oh, my gosh," whispered Becca. "That is too hilarious."

"This could be ridiculously hysterical at the right time," said Ellie. "Keep it under wraps, Mia. It has to be a last resort kind of thing. Mrs. 'G' is going to be watching everything."

A loud bell clanged three times from somewhere on the bridge. *"All hands on deck!"* the captain called to the crew. *"Prepare to dock and tie down!"* The engines slowed to a low hum as the boat slid toward the dock.

Click. *"We'll be at our docking point in a few minutes, folks,"* said the captain. *"Start headin' for the lower deck to collect your things. Meantime, you might catch a glimpse of some fish around the island that appear to be flying. They don't really fly. They just leap out of the water, spread their long fins and glide over the surface."* Click.

"What a way to travel," said Mia. "Just hold out your arms and sail!"

Mrs. Gunderson herded the class and chaperones to a spot below deck and again counted noses. "Just hold on kids. We'll let the rest of the passengers get off, and then it will be our turn. Keep a lid on it!"

Without much more than a gentle nudge, the boat made contact with the slip. Crew members of **STARSHIP II** jumped onto the dock and secured the vessel.

Chapter 37
Onward Campers!

Except for a couple of chaperones getting queasy and weak in the knees on the boat ride, everyone arrived at Cypress Cove in good spirits. Two college-aged students, working on their marine biology major, met the enthusiastic group at the landing. Their navy-blue polo shirts matched the ball caps they wore with the words, Campo del Mar embroidered in gold letters.

"Good morning, Lemon Grove students and chaperones. My name is Jason and this is Cathy. We'll be your instructors for the next three days. Drop your stuff here, kids, except for your lunch if you haven't already eaten it." He laughed.

"Our helpers will truck your things to camp and we'll sort everything there. Fall in behind me. We'll be hiking in to camp. Cathy and I will try to answer questions on the way. Absolutely stay on the trail and no running!"

Thirty students and five adults acknowledged the instructions, and the group began the 30-minute hike to camp. The trail worked its way across a steep ridge that overlooked the deep blue of a horseshoe shaped cove on the leeward side of the island.

"Get a load of that," said Spencer. "You can see clear to the bottom!"

"See any sharks?" asked Tank.

"Don't be stupid," said Zach, "they hide during the day."

"That's all you know," said Alex. "Sharks are always swimming. They have to, to stay alive." He kicked a stone ahead of him, sending it bouncing over the edge.

The trail gradually wound its way down to sea level where a large wooden lodge sat about 100 yards up from the beach. A long dock jutted out into the water where a flat pontoon boat was tied. Rows of kayaks lined the shore.

Beyond the lodge, among the island's native cherry trees, groups of tents were set up in circular patterns. Bathrooms and showers were clustered together, and an adult get-away-cabin was set up on the opposite side of the work-road where chaperones could catch a quiet moment for themselves or have a cup of coffee.

"When we reach the lodge, kids, gather 'round the picnic tables," said Cathy. "You can eat your lunch while Jason and I give you the lowdown on camp rules and clue you in on your classes."

"Can't get away from school," said Alex.

"Yeah, but this is different," said Zach. "We got all kinds of stuff to see and do. This ain't gonna be any regular ol' school."

"Hope we get to bunk together," said Tank. "I never been this far away from home and my own bed. Seems weird."

"Chill, Tank," said Spencer. "You always got Grampa Potter to hang with if we have to separate. Don't think about it right now. Man I'm so hungry I could eat my shirt."

When the last of the students reached the tables, they pulled out their lunches. With mouths full of food, it was possible for Jason and Cathy to speak without raised voices.

"You'll be divided into groups for study and exploration activities," said Jason. "Name your group after some kind of marine life like, The Dolphins, or Sharks, or Otters. You can figure that out with your group leader. The boys and girls tent sites are a short distance up the road. Close, but in separate areas. We'll assign those in a few minutes."

"Behind you," continued Cathy, "is our cafeteria and study hall. Mrs. Gunderson will help you create teams for serving and cleaning up at each meal. Everybody works here. No slackers! Over there," Cathy pointed across the maintenance road, "is the infirmary. If you get sick or hurt, the nurse will help you. Beyond the infirmary is our observatory and science lab."

"Will we ever get to be in the water?" asked Ellie.

"You bet," said Jason. "Snorkeling, kayaking, collecting information about the water, and identifying sea life and plants. Lots to do."

"Cool," said Tank. He looked over at Grampa Potter who held up two thumbs.

"Once you finish your lunch, kids," said Cathy, "we'll walk up the road to the tent area. Your belongings have been left up there, and your teacher will assign your sleeping quarters. I'll show you the showers and bathrooms while we hike up the road."

"Nightmare," said Mia. "This is the part I'm gonna hate. I don't think I'll ever take a shower while I'm here."

"Don't be such a prude," said Becca. "The biggest problem we'll have is getting Ellie away from the mirrors."

"That's what you think," said Ellie. "I'm *in* for this trip. I don't need to be too fancy."

Cathy and Jason marched the group up the hill toward the campsites. "There are wild pigs on the island," said Jason. "If you don't want them rummaging through your things and pooping in your tent, now's the time to dig out any candy, gum, or food from your bags. We don't want nighttime visitors."

Alex looked at Tank. "Get rid of the Twinkies, Tank."

"Shoot. That was my connection to life. Who do I give 'em to? You guys bring stuff?"

"I brought some gum," said Spencer reaching into his pocket. "There goes that." Becca's note was waded up with the five packs of bubble gum. *I still can't figure out what her stupid note is all about. Maybe we'll be on teams or something. Maybe I'll just pretend I lost it. No big deal.*

Ahead of the group were the canvas tents, six in each circle. The arrangement was constructed so that a chaperone could be within easy distance of rescue, night frights, or excessive chatter.

"Look you guys!" yelled Mia. "This *must* be the girl's side. Campsite 5. Right, Mrs. 'G'? It's a lot cleaner than the tents over there." She pointed to the circle of tents about twenty five feet away; some of which the cloth doors were hanging open or ripped in places.

"Right, girls," said Mrs. Gunderson. "Choose your tent and get yourselves settled while I take care of the boys. Be thinking of your group name."

"This is perfect," said Ellie. "There's a wood floor inside and four beds. Let's grab this tent. Hey, everyone!" She poked her head out of the tent and called to the rest of the scrambling girls. "What're we going to call ourselves?"

"For heaven's sake, Ellie. Let's just get organized first," said Becca. "We can figure that out later."

The girls arranged their sleeping bags across their chosen cots and fixed them for quick entry. Nights could be chilly on the island.

Duffle bags were opened, clothes sorted, and shoes placed under each bed. "This is some way to go to school," said Becca. "Don't ya love all the wild cherry trees?"

Mia picked up Spencer's 'treasure' and waved it at the girls in silence. "I'm putting it under my pillow until just the right moment. This could come in real handy," she whispered.

"What do you guys think about calling us *The Sea Stars*?" asked Ellie.

Chapter 38
Settling In

After bouncing on the worn and skinny mattresses, Zach, Spencer, Alex, and Tank played 'Rock, Paper, Scissors' to choose their cots. With no thought for neatness, they unrolled sleeping bags and crumpled pillows. Everything else was dumped on the floor or shoved under the sagging springs of their beds.

"So much for organizing," said Alex. "Hope we can remember whose stuff is what. I brought my brother's flashlight, and he'll be mighty 'ticked' if I lose it. Anybody see it?"

"It's on your cot," said Zach. "We're gonna need our flashlights when we come back from night class. That's a first. Night class I mean."

"Lose your light, Spence?" asked Tank. "What ya lookin' for anyway?"

"My flashlight's under my pillow," said Spencer. "I just can't find something else I brought. It'll turn up. No big deal."

"What is it?" asked Alex.

"Nothin'. Forget it," said Spencer. "Let's get the rest of the guys and figure out a name for our group." *Where did I put that? And here's that stupid note.*

"I like the name *Sharks*, or *Great Whites*," said Tank.

"As long as we're not Tuna fish. I can't stand that stuff," said Zach. What about callin' us *The Squids*?"

"Bring it up and we'll vote. Let's see what the rest of the guys are doing. We need to check the work list too," said Spencer. "Find out when we're on duty."

"Hope we get to *set* the tables instead of clean up," said Alex. "I do enough of that stuff at home."

The boys in Campsite 6 finally settled on calling themselves *The Orcas*, and as luck would have it, Tank, Alex, Spencer, and Zach got on the list for 'Clean Up', but not until the second day at dinner.

"Well, that's at least a break," said Tank. "Wonder what's for dinner tonight?"

"It better be good," said Zach. "I'm starving, and I gave all my snacks to Mrs. 'G', so there's not even a crumb around here. What's tonight's class about anyway?"

"The assignment book says something about *Anatomy of a Squid*. Dissecting and eating the dang thing. I think I'll puke if I have to do that," said Alex. "Shoot."

"Maybe we don't have to eat 'em," said Tank. "Just pretend. Who knows? Maybe they're good. Just pack a lot of ketchup on."

"You'd eat slugs if there was enough ketchup smeared all over 'em," said Spencer.

"Check it out, guys," said Zach gawking between the tents to Campsite 5. "The girls are actually sweeping the dirt! Fools. Why can't they just be regular old campers? Hey, Mia! You polishing the rocks next? You guys pick a name?"

Mia looked in their direction and stuck out her tongue. "Wouldn't you like to know?" she hollered. "Anything's better than what you nerds could think up. We're *The Sea Stars* for your information."

"Figures," said Alex. "Bet Ellie came up with that one."

"So," called Spencer, "it's *The Orcas* against *The Sea Stars*. We'll take you on at volley-ball after dinner. Beat you, too."

"You've lost your mind," said Mia. "Just wait. You'll never survive my serve. Besides, we've got class after dinner."

"How 'bout a game now then?" challenged Spencer. "Ask Mrs. 'G' if we can go down to the court."

"You letting everyone play?" asked Mia.

"Sure. It'll give us some practice for the next volley-ball war game," said Spencer.

"You're on, Mr. Orca. Don't whine when you lose."

Chapter 39
Learning the Ropes

In Campsite 5, the *Sea Stars* were in a frenzy of tent fixing. Mia, Ellie, and Becca had chosen a tent that gave them a clear view of the space occupied by Tank and company. They were prepared to keep an eye on the foursome.

"What's with the rope, Ellie? I mean stringin' it from one end of the tent to the other?" asked Mia. Ellie tied a sailor's knot high on the tent pole, stretched it across to the other tent pole and tied another knot.

"Makes perfect sense, Mia. Daddy taught me how to do this when we're on our boat. We can hang our clothes and towels on the rope. Keeps stuff off the floor. We won't be stepping on everything when we change." *Anyway, I want to look perfect.*

"Genius," said Becca. "And I can tie my mirror to the tent flap. That way we won't have to compete for bathroom space in the morning."

"I'm attaching nothing to anything," said Mia. "Not that I'd have anything in the first place. Anyway, the boys just challenged us to a before-dinner-volley-ball-game. You guys interested? Anyone can play that wants to."

"I'll get too sweaty," said Ellie. "Maybe tomorrow. Besides we've got class later, and I don't want to be taking a shower in that weird bathroom at night."

"Me neither," said Becca. "We're drawing names for study partners after dinner and I'd rather smell decent. *Especially if Spencer and I are partners!* After we dissect squid, we all might need a shower. That's just so gross."

"I heard the cook is frying them up for us. After class snack or something," said Mia. "They're actually pretty good. I've had 'em before. Just a little chewy."

"You can have *all* of mine," said Ellie. "I get the shivers just thinking about all those curly legs wiggling down my throat."

"They *are* dead you know, Ellie. So no volley-ball I take it?" said Mia.

"Next time," said Ellie. "Becca and me'll get this tent organized."

"I'll catch up with you guys later then," said Mia. "There's no way I'm going to let the guys think they can beat us. Anyways, I might even find out if they're tryin' to dream up any dumb ideas."

The boys stopped down the path and tossed the volley-ball back and forth. They waited to see if they had any challengers. Mia rounded up a few other *Sea Stars*, signaled to the boys, and they all took off for the volley-ball court.

"Ha! Look at those guys *try* to run," said Mia, turning to the girls behind her. "Let's show 'em who's in charge!"

"Hey, Mia! Where's Ellie? Ain't she playin'?" Tank stopped and waited for Mia to catch up.

"She's still foolin' around setting up the tent with Becca. Stringin' ropes for clothes and stuff," said Mia.

"Ropes?" asked Tank, falling in step with Mia.

"Yeah. Supposed to keep the clothes off the floor. Towels dry. Whatever. She strung it across the tent. She's such a neat-freak you know."

"She thinks of everythin'," said Tank. He smiled and jogged off. "Get ready to be whupped, Mia. You girls are toast."

"Fools!" shouted Mia. "You guys will be *French* toast when we get through with you. Who serves first?"

Chapter 40
Anatomy of a Squid and Other Dark Tales

After dinner, the dining hall was arranged for the evening class. A bucket of small dead squid sat near the front of the cafeteria covered in a blanket of wet seaweed. While chaperones directed, the study groups spread newspapers on table tops to absorb any spillage of guts and gore.

"I don't know how anyone can do this disgusting stuff right after dinner," said Ellie. "The whole thing is gag-worthy."

"Oh, come on, Ellie. This is science, and you have to admit dinner *was* pretty good," said Becca. "Main dish and all you can eat?"

"Got that right," said Tank. "I got a whoppin' belly ache. Too much cornbread and chocolate milk." He belched long and loud.

"Gross. That's just rude, Tank. I thought you were getting over that stuff," said Becca.

Grampa Potter heard the obnoxious sound erupting from Tank, shook his head and turned thumbs down. Tank shrugged and nodded. *I get it. I get it.*

Luck of the draw made Ellie study partners with Tank, Zach and Mia. Spencer drew Becca's name as his partner and they were joined by the Meyer twins.

"I think I get your note now, Becca," said Spencer. "Study partners. Why didn't you just come out and ask me?"

"I didn't know if you'd be okay with it," said Becca. "I just wanted you to know that I'd like us to be partners." *Besides, you're cute*, she thought.

"I know how much you love science and I thought it would be fun to work together since I like science, too." *Shut up, Becca! Say no more. That was really dumb.* She fumbled with the papers in front of her and hoped Spencer wasn't staring at her.

"Well, who wouldn't want to partner with the smartest girl in class?" said Spencer.

Becca looked over her glasses at Spencer. *That isn't exactly what I had in mind, you big dope.* "Maybe you'd rather hang with Tank and those guys," she said. "I can trade with someone."

"Nah. They'll be fine. Ellie's no dummy," said Spencer. "She'll make 'em work. I want to see those guys squirm when *SHE* directs everything. Care if Alex comes over here with us? He can draw all the parts of the squid really good."

"What can I say?" said Becca, trying not to show her disappointment. *You'll just talk to him the whole time and ignore me. Thanks a lot Spence.*

Spencer wandered over to get Alex and passed the bucket of squid. When he turned around, Tank was at his side.

"You see what I see?" whispered Spencer, pointing to the pile of wet seaweed. He pretended to twist an imaginary moustache. "There's a plan forming in my head as we speak. Tell you later."

Tank elbowed Spencer and walked back to the tables. *Yer looking for trouble, Spence. Better not.* He glanced at Alex and Zach and raised both hands in submission. *I'm out of this one.*

At last the interns showed up. They carried plastic bins filled with dissection tools, hand lenses, and paper towels.

"Okay, group," said Jason. "Find your partners and sit yourselves down. Cathy and I will be passing out the squid. One per group." Jason swung the bucket of squid to the table top and removed the seaweed.

"Just observe your specimen," said Cathy, "and then we'll talk about the little cephalopods. If you manage a successful dissection, the cook will fry up the edible parts for us, and you'll get to try the tasty morsels. But first, we follow Jason's directions."

Cathy and Jason, along with the chaperones passed out the limp mollusks and placed them carefully in the center of each group, legs, tentacles and head extended as if they were swimming. Mrs. Gunderson passed out the baskets of tools.

"Eeeew," said Ellie. "They stink! And they're all slimy. I'm not touching that thing."

"Cool. Look at their eyes." Tank was ready to pick it up when Zach smacked his hand.

"Leave it, Tank," said Zach. "Let's see what we got to do first. Since you like to write so much, Ellie, you be the recorder. Just watch. Me and Tank'll do all the dissecting stuff."

"Oh, no you don't you guys," said Mia. "I get to do some cutting stuff, too. You can't have all the fun."

"Go for it, Mia," said Ellie. "I'll be happy to watch. I'm going to barf if I have to keep smelling this thing."

"Okay, scientists," said Jason. "Now that you've had a chance to do an observation, hands up for what you found."

The students' examination of the specimen and instructor discussion yielded information about its mantle, legs, tentacles, eyes, and mouth. A new respect for the ocean mollusk was created when the youngsters discovered how it could change color, move by jet propulsion, tear food with its beak, ward off predators by shooting out a black inky substance, and that it had not just one, but three hearts.

"Interestingly, the eyes have lenses that can open and close like cameras or telescopes," said Jason. "In fact, the giant squid has the largest eyeball in the animal kingdom. Like the size of a basketball!"

"No way!" Tank shouted. "That's some eyeball."

"Jason really likes to say that," said Cathy, laughing. "Now, look at the long narrow part of the body. That's the mantle. Inside, there's a plastic-like structure that holds the mantle and protects the intestines. Gently pull it out with the intestines and disconnect the ink sack. Take turns dipping the spine-like structure into the ink and see if you can write a message to your partners."

"Look, guys," said Mia, "here's that spine thing. You can almost see through it."

"Yeah. And it's pointy," said Tank. "Let's see if I can write something with it." Tank dipped the end of it into the black ink and scrawled his initials.

"Hey, give it over," said Zach. "Let me try."

Ellie held her nose and drew a diagram of the limp white blob resting in front of her. "See if you can find the hearts," she said, still holding her nose.

The group at Spencer's table found the internal structure that held out the mantle, but unfortunately, Spencer squeezed the ink sack which sent the black fishy liquid splattering all over himself and the twins. They went running to Mrs. Gunderson in tears.

Becca looked up from her notes and glared at Spencer. "Why," she growled, "did you do that? Now we won't be able to do that experiment. And don't tell me it was an accident."

"Well, it was."

"Oh, sure. Now what am I supposed to write? *Spencer ACCIDENTLY popped the ink sack?*"

Alex was sketching so intently that he hardly said a word. "Who cares, Becca? This thing is awesome. I've sketched the mantle and tentacles. Did you see all the little suction cups on 'em? I didn't know they have legs *and* tentacles."

He stopped sketching when Instructor Cathy spoke up. "Right where the legs and tentacles meet the mantle," said Cathy, "you can feel a hard lump. That would be the beak. Gently cut the legs and tentacles off at that point and set them aside. Right above the eyes, cut the mantle away and set it with the tentacles."

Each group managed to separate the tentacles from the mantle and locate the beak just below the eyes. "Wow!" said Alex. "This looks just like my parakeet's beak. That would really hurt if it bit ya."

"The beak is the only indigestible part of the squid," said Jason. "They've been found intact in the bellies of fish."

Mrs. Gunderson and the Chaperones picked up the severed legs and mantles and took them to the kitchen. "While Cooky gets our squid ready to taste, we need to clean up," said Cathy. "Then you can have your midnight snack. I'd say we had a very successful lesson."

Spencer grabbed the opportunity to help with the clean-up and watched where the remains of the seaweed were placed. He offered to help with taking out the trash. When he found the damp seaweed, he wrapped a pile of it in a piece of newspaper, set it down beside the steps, and sauntered back into the cafeteria, smiling.

Chapter 41
Careful What You Wish For

"Mrs. Gunderson?" Spencer tapped her on the shoulder. "I feel pretty slimy with squid guts all over me. Can I go get a shower?" Spencer had retrieved the seaweed and slipped it under the back of his shirt, but now a cold liquid began dripping down his pant leg making him appear badly in need of a bathroom.

"Sure, Spencer. Take someone with you, though. It's dark. Looks like you need to hurry. I'll send one of the chaperones up in a few minutes. Have your flashlight?"

"Yeah." He danced. "I just need to get my towel and stuff, and then I'll hit the showers."

Spencer gave himself some internal 'atta boy' encouragement and grabbed Alex and Zach. "C'mon you guys. We gotta hurry." Three flashlights lit the trail to the campsite as the boys moved at warp speed toward the tents.

"What the heck you doin', Spence?" Alex was more than a little concerned about the plan brewing in Spencer's head but kept up the spirited sprint. "You're gonna get us in trouble again." Mrs.

Gunderson's voice rang in his ears. "*You'll be sent home if you cause any kind of mischief.*"

"This seaweed is cold and it's getting me all wet," said Spencer.

"So what *are* you doing with it?" Zach punched out each word as the hill grew steeper and breathing became harder.

"I figured out how to get the girls good. With your help, of course. We need to split up when we get to camp," said Spencer. "If we do it right, no one will know it was us," said Spencer.

"Where've I heard that before? I don't like the sound of this." Alex remembered the last time those exact words were uttered by Spencer.

"So here's what we do," said Spencer. "One of you guys grab my towel and head for the showers. Hang my towel over the door and turn on the water. When someone shows up, pretend I'm showering and you're waitin' for me. You can do that. Right?" Spencer shined his flashlight at Zach.

"Okay," said Zach. "I'll go, but this better be darn good. Shame Tank's not here."

"He wanted no part of this, but *he's* the one that told me about Ellie's clothesline."

"What clothesline?" asked Zach.

"You'll see. Just wait."

"I'm staying at the tent," said Alex. "If I'm there, it won't look so suspicious." *Maybe I can escape trouble if there is any.*

"Okay," said Spencer. "You might be right on that one. Hold down the fort 'til I get back. Zach, once the chaperone checks that I'm showering, and he leaves, turn off the water at get back here with my towel. I'll pretend to be hanging it up."

"If we get caught, Spence, you know what'll happen," said Zach.

The pace slowed as the boys swung into their campsite. "Here's my towel, Zach-man. Get down to the showers."

Spencer sprinted over to the girls' tent and groped overhead for the clothesline Ellie had strung. Alex couldn't stand the secrecy and followed at a safe distance. He watched the whole prank unfold. "Hurry up, Spence!" he whispered. "I hear everyone comin' up the hill. We'll be invaded in seconds!"

"Done! I'm done, Alex." Spencer and Alex jogged back to the boys' area. Spencer was still damp and smelly from the squid ink and seaweed. "I'll hide under my cot. You sit on yours and look like you're gettin' your toothbrush or somethin' and just listen for the screaming. Ha. This ought to be good."

Spencer squeezed under the cot next to the rumpled assortment of clothes he dumped and waited. *Maybe I'll find my little buddy under here. What in the heck happened to it?*

Mia was the first to reach the girl's tent. She ducked under the flap, her back turned to the inside so she could prove she was once again *'the winner'*, and held the flaps open. Becca and Ellie were close behind her. They tore into the tent each trying to be ahead of the other. Mia hopped in. Then it began.

"Yiiiii!" Ellie screamed.

"OW! What the . . .!" Becca flailed her arms in the air, pulling the seaweed laden clothesline on top of the three of them.

"Pffft!" Mia spit at the slimy wet things hitting her in the mouth. "THIS IS WAR!" shouted Mia. "Just wait! If you did this, Spencer Johnson, you'll get yours tomorrow for sure!" *Idiot!*

Chapter 42
Now You've Done It!

Mrs. Gunderson ran to the girl's tent along with some of the other 'Sea Stars'. "Good grief! What happened? Are you all right?" She pulled the seaweed off the girls and wound the rope into a bundle.

"Seaweed? Where've I seen this before? Someone has some mighty big explaining to do," she said to no one in particular.

As the story unfolded at camp, the chaperone assigned to shower duty sat next to Zach in the washroom and chatted.

"Spencer's been in there an awfully long time. Someone else might want to shower before the water turns cold. Spencer?" he called. "Time to get out." No answer. "I don't hear anything. You sure he's okay? Hey, Spencer. Time's up."

Zach just shrugged his shoulders and looked sheepishly at the chaperone and the limp towel covering the doorway. "What can I say? Spencer likes long showers," said Zach.

A quick glance under the door exposed the truth. No feet. "Zach, what's going on? Nobody's in there. What's this all about? Turn off the water and get that towel. We're going to have a little talk with Mrs. Gunderson."

Here it comes, thought Zach. *I'm going home for sure. Or maybe jail. Thanks Spence.*

Mrs. Gunderson was now more concerned than angry. "So where *is* Spencer, Alex? And where's Zach?" "Spence's still at the showers with Zach." Alex lied, uncomfortable to be placed in such an awkward position.

"Afraid not," said the chaperone, entering the girls'area. "Zach is right here with me, but no Spencer."

"What do you boys know about this?" Mrs. Gunderson used her I-mean-it lecture voice. "It had better be good. We'll deal with the outcome later, but first we need to find Spencer before I call your parents and put you all on a boat headed home!"

Spencer heard the rising commotion and decided that he couldn't let Alex and Zach take the heat alone. He crawled out from under the cot and high-tailed it to the girls' area. "Here I am, Mrs. Gunderson. Guess I . . . we're in trouble. Right?"

"You had better believe it, boys." Her voice was like wind before a storm.

Tank could hear the anger in Mrs. Gunderson's voice. He wandered over to the group with Grampa Potter. "At least I wasn't in on this one, Grampa. All I did was tell the guys about the clothesline in the girl's tent."

"Oh, really? That's guilt by association," said Grampa.

"What the heck does that mean?"

"That makes you part of the story, Tank."

"Just 'cause I told them about the rope?"

"Yup."

"But, that ain't fair," Tank protested. "I didn't tell them to pull this."

"You didn't have to. You provided the opening for the prank. Let's see what Mrs. Gunderson comes up with before we jump to conclusions. She's firm, but she *is* fair," said Grampa. "Some lessons are hard learned. Looks like it may take awhile for you boys to figure that out."

"Geez," said Tank. "Here I go again. Right in the middle of trouble. Dang!"

Once the facts were sorted out, Mrs. Gunderson made her decision. "Okay boys, I'm not sending you home, BUT . . . all four of you will be on detention tomorrow morning. That means you'll miss the snorkeling and oceanography classes. One of the chaperones will monitor you, and if the instructors want you to do kitchen duty, you're on. I want a written apology to the girls, too. Got it? We've only got tomorrow and the following morning before we go home. We'll see about the afternoon classes. Think you can keep yourselves under control that long?"

"Yes, Ma'am," they muttered, avoiding each other's eyes.

The group wrapped up the evening with S'mores and campfire songs. Then it was off to bed. Sleep didn't come easy for the boys in Spencer's tent. Conversation carried an angry tone.

"You and your stupid ideas, Spence," groaned Alex. "Now we have to miss one of the best classes of this whole trip."

"Yeah," agreed Zach. "I was really lookin' forward to the snorkel event. Shouldn't a listened to your dumb idea."

"All I did was tell you guys about Ellie's rope," said Tank, "and look what happened to me. You got me in trouble again. Story of my life. Thanks for nothin' Spence."

"Okay, okay. I got it guys. Sorreeee. It didn't go quite the way I planned. We still got another night class tomorrow with dino . . . dino . . ."

"Dinoflagellates and bioflourescent plankton." Zach finished the sentence.

". . . And kayaking the next day," Spencer continued. "How come you know so much about those dino things anyway, Zach?"

"I don't. I just like to say the words."

"You're weird."

Spencer shined his flashlight at the tent ceiling and made small circles with the beam. Soon all four lights shone on the top of the tent in a flashlight war. In the next tent, someone was already snoring. Little by little, flashlights were extinguished and all was quiet.

I wish I had my little buddy right now. What in the heck happened to it? It just disappeared. Spencer drifted off.

In the girl's tent, Mia was silly-singing a song about Spencer and waving his lost treasure in the air. "Since we're on kitchen duty for breakfast tomorrow, we can hang this up near the front of the cafeteria with a BIG sign: 'THIS BELONGS TO SPENCER JOHNSON'. What a burn!"

Becca and Ellie giggled. "I can't wait to see Spencer's face," said Ellie. "He's *really* got it coming."

"Think we'll get in trouble?" asked Becca.

"Nah," said Mia, "and so what if we do. It'll be worth it. 'Night everybody."

Why does Spencer have to be so weird, thought Becca. *Maybe I don't like him after all. What a jerk. He ruins everything.*

Chapter 43
Lost and Found

Mia slapped at the alarm clock—6:30. "Hey, wake up you guys! It's our turn to set up for breakfast. Ellie! Becca! Get up. Breakfast! The class will be down before you know it, and we've got to get a sign ready."

The girls had slept in their clothes so they could stay in their sleeping bags 'til the last possible minute. Mia slipped on her flip-flops and headed down the hill with Spencer's personal item tucked inside her sweatshirt.

Becca ran a brush through her hair, and hollered at Ellie as she swung open the tent flaps. "Come on, Ellie. Move it! You look fine. Do your make-up later."

Ellie yawned, zipped out of her sleeping bag and shuffled to the mirror. "No way. I can't go to the cafeteria looking like this." She mumbled at the sideways hanging mirror. "Tank'll think I slept in a tree with a bunch of squirrels." *If he even cares.*

Ellie brushed out the snarls, grabbed a scrunchy, and pulled her hair into a pony tail. "Better," she said, talking to the mirror again. She pinched her cheeks a few times and applied a dab of lip gloss.

She talked to the mirror. "So what do you expect at 6:30 AM? Miracles?"

Becca and Mia had already set eight of the tables by the time Ellie arrived. "Brought the markers," she said, yawning. "Where's the paper?"

"The cook gave us a piece of butcher paper," said Mia. "Tape and tacks, too."

"Let's put it on the bulletin board where everyone comes in," said Becca. "Then we can put this raggedy thing right in the middle."

"I can't wait to see the expression on Spencer's face," said Ellie, taking the paper and markers to a back table. At the top in large block letters she wrote:

DID YOU LOSE THIS SPENCER?

Then she drew a large flowery circle in the middle with arrows pointing to the spot where Spencer's toy would be placed. The girls taped the poster onto the board and tacked a small and tattered teddy bear smack in the center of the circle.

"That little piece of silk pinned around its neck looks like it could have been part of a baby blanket," said Becca. "Spencer's blue baby blanky maybe?"

"Duh, Becca. Ya think?" said Mia. "You're prob'ly right. That bear is pretty ratty looking. Like it's been around for a thousand years."

The girls stood back and admired their work. "Very cool," said Ellie. "Let the fun begin."

"Make it a respectable line," Mrs. Gunderson called over her shoulder as the group ambled down the hill to breakfast. "We aren't a herd of buffalo, off to a watering hole."

"Man, I'm starving," said Tank.

"Count me in. I could eat a horse," said Zach. "I had nightmares last night because of you, Spence. You and your stupid ideas."

"Better eat lots, you guys. Detention could be deadly," said Alex. "Nothin' to say, Spence?"

"Just leave me alone. I'm not hungry anyways."

Howls of laughter began as the first set of campers entered the mess hall. Spencer could faintly hear his name being bantered about inside.

What's goin' on? he wondered. *Everyone's prob'ly still mad at me for messin' up last night.*

When he reached the entrance, he spotted the glaring source of everyone's laughter. He spun around nearly knocking Tank over and ran.

"Ah, come on, Spence," called Mia. "Come back. It's just a joke!"

Tank ran after him. Mrs. Gunderson grabbed Alex and Zach by their shirt tails. "Let Tank go. I'll tell Jason and Cathy what happened. We'll find him."

Then she turned toward the girls. "Could there be any possibility that you ladies know something about this fiasco? Looks like the morning detention group is growing."

Becca's eyes went all blurry as tears began to form. *Maybe we went too far this time.*

Chapter 44
True Confessions

"Wait, Spence! Wait up!" Tank ran after Spencer.

About 50 yards down the path, Spencer took a quick left and headed for Silver Spur Mine which the class had explored earlier complete with miners' hats and front mounted lights. Grampa Potter followed at a slower pace but within easy range to see where they were headed.

Spencer worked his way into the mine a ways and slumped down on the cold rock floor, head between his knees, and cried. Tank was a few steps behind.

"Spence? Where are you?" Tank's voice echoed into the darkness. Hand over hand he inched along the wall.

"Go away. Leave me alone."

"Come on, Spence. Ain't no big deal. Ya just didn't expect it. That's all."

"That's what YOU think, stupid. Now everyone thinks I'm just a big baby."

"Right. That's eggzakly what everyone'll think if you don't get your stupid head together." Tank eased toward the sound of Spencer's voice and sat down next to him.

Grampa Potter reached the entrance to the mine. He could hear the boys' echoing conversation. When Cathy and Jason came whipping down the hill, he held up a hand motioning for them to stop and put a finger to his lips. The three of them stood together and waited.

Spencer wiped his face on his sweatshirt sleeve and stared into the dark. "This sucks, man. How can I . . . ?"

"Shut up, Spence. Let me tell *you* somethin', and if *you* tell everyone, ain't no skin off my nose. Least ways not any more."

"Can't be as bad as me."

"Try me," said Tank. "Know how I never got to stay over at anybody's house?"

"Yeah?"

"Know why?"

"No."

"Because I wet the bed."

Silence.

"YOU? YOU wet the bed? Tank, you're almost eleven! My dumb sister doesn't even wet the bed any more."

"Told you it was major." Tank felt embarrassed and relieved at the same time. His secret was out. Now, no matter what, everyone would know.

"So, how come you got to come camping?"

"Somethin' happened after my accident. When old "Pottsy" said he'd be my Grampa, I just quit. Haven't had a bed-wettin' problem since. Go figure."

"That explains a lot," said Spencer. "Guess that is kind of embarrassing."

"It's dang embarrassin'!" howled Tank. "Now you can go spread *that* around if it helps. But, I bet lots of kids have stuffed animals.

Ain't nothin' wrong with that. So come on. Pretend you don't give a darn. Just let it blow over."

Grampa Potter looked at Cathy and Jason. "Guess things are gonna work out okay," he said. "Let's see how we can play this down. I'm really proud of Tank. He did a good thing. I'll wait for the boys. You two head on back to camp."

"I have an idea," said Jason. He turned to Cathy. "Let's get back to the mess hall."

Breakfast was nearly over, tables were being cleared and Mrs. Gunderson had taken down the sign and the ragged teddy bear. "May I hang on to it, Mrs. 'G'?" asked Becca. "I'll make sure we apologize when we give it back to Spencer." *Never expected he would get so upset.*

"And that will be the end of all this nonsense, right?"

"For sure, Mrs. 'G'. No more games." She tucked the bear in her pocket safely out of sight. *I want to be the one to give it back. That was pretty cold.*

Jason and Cathy stood on a cafeteria bench and talked to the group about *their* most embarrassing moments growing up. "So, before we break up into our lesson groups, this is what we can do," said Jason. "Mr. Potter should be back with the boys soon, so no smart remarks. Keep yourselves under control, and just follow our lead."

Unnoticed, Grampa Potter, Tank, and Spencer slipped into the cafeteria and sat down at the back. "What are they doing?" whispered Spencer.

"No idea," said Tank. "Some kind of exercise? Hands up? Stand up? Darned if I know."

"Okay, group. Confession time. Hands up if you ever threw up in the classroom." Around the room a few hands went up accompanied by nervous giggling. "Hands up if you spy on your sister or brother." Again a few hands and laughter. "Good," said Jason. "You're playing fair. Hands up if you ever cheated on a spelling test." More hands. "Up with the hands if you sometimes sleep with a stuffed animal."

Spencer's face flushed as nearly half the room, Jason *and* Cathy raised their hands.

"And now the clincher. Hands up if you ever wet your bed," he half whispered. Slowly, for those who could, hands went up around the room, including Jason's. "Yep," said Jason, "I was one of those. Wet the bed 'til I was 11. So, looks like we've all been embarrassed by stupid secrets we're afraid to tell. Can we forget about this now and get on to more marine biology?"

The room exploded in cheers.

"But," Cathy interrupted, "I'll see all of you who earned detention, everyone else, off to snorkeling."

"Some morning, huh?" said Mr. Potter. "It's only 8:30 and I'm already beat. Want me to chaperone the detainees, Mrs. Gunderson? I'm way beyond a wet suit and snorkeling."

"You're on," said Mrs. Gunderson. "I'll need the rest of the chaperones in the water with the kids. Be sure to catch a well-deserved break if you can. You'll need it. Sure hope this trip hasn't discouraged you from riding herd on these youngsters. It can be overwhelming."

"Wouldn't have missed it for the world," he said. *I have a lot to be thankful for.*

"I'll be ready for kayaking later."

Chapter 45
Just Do It

The weary detainees finished their morning duties. Grampa Potter pointed to a table and motioned for them to sit. He wiped his forehead and went into the cafeteria to get drinks for the group. They twiddled and stared at each other, no one wanting to be the first to speak about the cause of their detention.

Finally, Becca took Spencer's tattered bear from her pocket and propped it in the middle of the table. Spencer ignored it, pretending not to be interested.

"We're really sorry, Spence," said Becca, breaking the stare-down. "I . . . um, *we* didn't mean to make you feel so bad. It was all Mia's idea, you know, to get you back for the stupid seaweed trick."

"Sure. Blame it all on me. You guys didn't try to stop me."

"Oh, get over it, Mia," said Ellie. "You *know* you're always the one with the BIG ideas. You and Spence and Tank. I'm through with all this stupid stuff. Before we get into any more trouble, think we can call a truce? I really don't want to miss the rest of my time here."

The boys looked at each other. "Well," said Tank, "I think we can call it quits, for now anyway."

"Okay by me," said Alex.

"No," said Becca. "Not just for now. From now on. Grow up. We've been doing this since first grade. It's time to think about next year and middle school and harder classes and . . ."

"And any reputation we have left," Mia conceded. "So truce?"

She plunked her hand down on the table and resigned herself to the inevitable. Tank put his hand on Mia's. Then, one over the other, the group stacked their hands in ritual agreement.

"Truce." They said in unison.

Tank held on to Mia's hand. "Let . . . *go*, Tank." She pulled it out from under his, in no mood to thumb-wrestle if that was his intention.

The cafeteria door opened and Grampa Potter came down the stairs carrying a tray with eight glasses of lemonade.

"Here you go kids. Too bad you missed out on snorkeling." He didn't have to say more about the lost opportunity. The silence that followed was enough to let him know they understood. He took a long swig of lemonade and set his glass down. "So, if all goes well, kayaking this afternoon, right?"

"Right," said Spencer, picking up the bedraggled bear and stuffing it in his pocket. *Guess you'll be on my shelf when I get home. No more traveling for you, BearBear.*

"You coming too, Grampa Potter?" asked Zach.

"I'd like to try it."

"Awesome," said Tank. "This is gonna be so cool!"

"Finally. I'll get to wear my new bathing suit," said Ellie.

"Gee. I can hardly wait." Mia was tired of Ellie's clothes-horse mentality.

Becca glared at Mia over her sunglasses. "Sarcasm doesn't become you, my dear. Shut-up and drink your lemonade. Let's have some real fun for a change."

"I'm starving," said Alex. "I hope everyone gets back here pretty soon."

"You're in luck, genius," said Mia. "I see 'em coming up the hill right now."

Chapter 46
So What Happened?

Lunch included a rambling conversation about wet suits, masks, snorkels, and sea life. The seven trouble-makers quizzed their friends concerning the missed snorkeling adventure.

"So what did you guys do?" asked Zach, attempting to speak through an enormous bite of hamburger.

"You tell 'em, Joan," said one of the twins. "I am starving." She brushed a strand of wet hair from her eyes and reached for a piece of pizza. "Yum . . . heaven," she muttered.

Joan nibbled at the skewered piece of meat on the end of her fork. "Well," she began, "We had to put on wet suits, funny looking caps, and booties. We looked ridiculous. Flippers were the tricky part. George tripped over his and landed face first in the sand!"

"That's no surprise," said Mia. "His feet are the biggest things I've ever seen."

"Then," Joan continued, "I got a mouthful of water through my snorkel and nearly choked to death."

"She's just being dramatic," said Jan. "We *all* got water in our mouths."

"But the grossest thing was when we had to spit into our masks and smear it around on the glass part."

"Hey, I'm eating. That is *totally* disgusting," said Ellie. "Why?"

"To keep the mask from fogging up. And it really worked!"

Spencer and Tank didn't stop to talk until they had picked every morsel from their plates.

"So what did you guys see?" asked Spencer. He looked at Tank and pointed to Tank's chin where remnants of his lunch were still suspended on little strings of cheese. Tank reached for his napkin, grabbed four more cookies and poured another glass of milk.

"It was so cool," said Jan. "We found an octopus hiding in the rocks. It waved its tentacles all around and swam off when we got too close. It even 'inked' us! That was way funny, and its eyes were really big."

"And," interrupted Joan, "we saw an orange and blue fish, some volcano barnacles, sea stars, worms, and those big snails the Indians made bowls and scrappers out of."

"Snails? I thought those were only in the garden," said Tank.

"Sea snails," said Joan. "You know. Aba . . . Aba . . ."

"You mean abalone?" Ellie had tasted the delicacy at a restaurant where her parents liked to go. "That's a snail? Gross! I'm never eating that again!"

By the end of the meal there wasn't a crumb of anything identifiable left on the serving plates.

"Looks like hunger was a great cook," said Mrs. Gunderson. She walked by to check on the detainees and excuse individual tables. "Rest up, kids. We'll be kayaking at 2 o'clock. You feeling up to this, Mr. Potter?"

"I wouldn't miss it, Mrs. Gunderson," he said. He took a welcome sip of coffee and handed a second cup to her.

"Bless you, Mr. Potter." She closed her eyes, breathed in its dark fragrance, and took a long sip of the rejuvenating brew. *Peace, quiet for a moment. Thank you, Lord.*

Chapter 47
The Race to Pelican Rock

After a brief rest, the class met at the beach next to the boat locker. “Gather ‘round everyone for kayaking lessons.” Jason sang out instructions while Cathy stood by like a statue, holding a double-ended paddle in one hand and a life vest in the other. Students squinted in the bright sun fidgeting while Jason talked. They were anxious to get going. When he had finished, Cathy took over and demonstrated how to put on the life vest and how to use the paddle.

“Getting into the kayak is usually no problem,” she said, “but getting *back* in if you fall out while you are in the water is a different story. Watch!”

She paddled out a short distance stroking the water first on one side and then the other. The small craft moved in a straight line. “Paddling several times on one side makes the kayak turn,” she said, coming about and shouting to everyone on shore. She demonstrated the turn again and purposely tipped over. The boat hung upside down, and for a few seconds Cathy disappeared, causing a horrified reaction in the students.

With a splash, she popped up like a fishing bob, free of the boat which remained bottom side up.

"That's scary," said Becca. "I don't think I like this."

"Your vest'll bring you up," said Ellie, using her sailing expertise. "Not to worry."

"How's she gonna turn it over?" asked Tank.

"Just keep quiet and watch, Tanker." *Tank-er? Where'd that come from?* Mia was listening intently, anxious to get into the kayak and take off.

"*Your* paddle is attached to the hull by a tether," said Cathy, keeping her voice raised, "so it won't get away from you when you tip. Besides, it floats. Then, just place one arm over the bottom of the kayak and pull it toward you. With a little tug, it should right itself. Pull yourself up onto the kayak and lay over the mid-section. Get your bottom into the hull, scoot back in the seat, and you're in business again." Her recovery was flawless. "Now everybody, shove off and hop in. We're all going to do the 'tip and flip'."

"This is crazy," said Spencer, wading into the cold water. "There ought to be a better way to get wet."

"Right," said Mia, "so don't do it if you're afraid." *Big chicken.*

Zach and Alex pushed their kayaks into the bay. "This sure ain't river water," said Alex. "It's dang cold. I'm not doing any flipping thing if I can help it."

"Me neither. We'll warm up once we get our muscles firing." Zach responded with bravado. "Wonder how fast can these things go? Think there's sharks?"

"Sharks? They're out there somewhere, stupid," said Alex. "What did you say that for? Now that's all I'll think about. Thanks a lot." *Maybe if I think about Ellie, I won't think about getting eaten.*

In spite of the teetering and wobbling, everyone managed to

get into a kayak and straggle out into the bay. They collided and bumped into each other like bumper cars at a carnival ride. Paddles tangled, boats went in circles, and no one seemed to be getting any momentum. A whistle blew.

"Okay everyone. Stop where you are and tip over."

Jason and Cathy watched the melee. Mia pretended to tip, almost going over then righting herself. She simply watched how it was done. *Piece of cake. I can do that. No sweat.*

With considerable struggle for some, and a little help for others, they managed to get back into their boats. Tank was first to get back in his kayak. No problem for a boy who had grown taller and stronger during the school year.

"Come on, paddlers. You'll warm up once you get moving. You've been divided into color groups," said Cathy, "so follow your leader."

"Ya-hoo!" shouted Tank. He and Mia were in the orange group led by Jason. Grampa Potter paddled up beside Tank.

"How's it goin', son?"

"Great! I'm just tryin' to keep up with Jason. It's out to Pelican Rock and back. You doin'okay?"

"You bet, Tank. I'll meet you on the way back."

"Cool." Tank spun in a circle, corrected, and headed after Jason. Mia was on his heels.

"Race?" Mia hollered after Tank. She wasn't about to be outdone by anyone, especially Tank.

"You'll never catch me, Mia. I got lots more muscles than you'll ever hope to have."

"Ha! And they're all in your big fat head, buster. I've always been ten times faster than you. See ya!" She dipped the paddle deep from side to side, leaving Tank in her wake.

Becca and Ellie gave her a thumbs-up as she slid by. They weren't among the 'tip and flippers'. The decision was based on Ellie's hair and Becca's new sunglasses.

"Looks like Mia's done this before," said Becca.

"Typical. Mia can't pass up a challenge if it has anything to do with the boys," said Ellie. "My arms are getting tired. Let's wait for Alex and Zach. They're just poking along. What's with them?"

"I heard Zach say something about sharks and Alex freaked. They're prob'ly just watching for *something from beneath*." Becca used her dramatic voice to emphasize the danger.

"You mean they're scared. Big, brave Zach." Ellie laughed. "That's classic."

"No lolly-gagging, girls," called out Mrs. Gunderson. "Get a move on!"

Ellie waved in response. "Pretend we're having trouble and spin around a lot," said Ellie. "That way everyone else will be around the rock and on their way back. We can fake it."

"For a sailor, you can come up with the stupidest ideas," said Becca. "Look at Spencer. He's going really good." *He looks so cute in his Kayak, and sunglasses, and white sun- stuff on his nose.* Becca was lost in her private thoughts.

"Hello? Earth to Becca." Ellie's voice jerked Becca from her day-dream. "It's a miracle! Alex and Zach are actually moving this way. The two brave shark hunters," Ellie announced, laughing at their awkwardness. She looked around for the other paddlers. "Becca, look!"

Becca strained to see what Ellie was pointing at. "Oh, my gosh. It's Mia and Tank. Looks like Mia's ahead by a whole kayak."

"Not that. Ahead! Look ahead of Mia! It's a fin! I see a fin!" Ellie's yelling startled everyone including Alex and Zach who were pulling alongside the girls. Grampa Potter turned his kayak and raced toward Mia and Tank. Jason and Cathy were behind all the stragglers which separated them from the two racers and the impending disaster.

Mia spotted the slightly curved fin—or was it two? slicing through the water ahead of her. She slowed almost to a stop, turning her kayak. Tank kept coming, driving his paddle with a vengeance. It only took seconds. Tank's kayak rammed into Mia and over she went.

"Mia!" he yelled. "I'm sorry. I'm sorry. Where are you? Why'd you stop?"

When she didn't surface, Tank yanked off his vest and rolled into the water. The salt stung his eyes, but he could see Mia hanging under the kayak. Her leg was tangled in the tether; the rope snagged on a piece of kelp. She was struggling to free herself. The vest kept lifting her into the hull and trapping her. Tank worked the seaweed and tether from Mia's leg and pulled her away from the craft.

Mia's life jacket lifted her. She was in a panic, gasping for air, and grabbing for Tank. The fin was gone.

Tank wrestled Mia onto her back and held her. Her head rested on his shoulder. Her heart pounded. Her vest supported both of them. When Jason and Grampa Potter reached the distressed paddlers, they righted the kayaks and got Tank and Mia into one of them. Jason knew the kayak could hold the weight of two kids, but there was too much weight to place an adult and child together. So there they were, Tank and Mia.

"Keep an eye on them," he hollered to Cathy. "We'll tow them in."

As they were being towed, Tank held a shivering Mia against

his chest, trying to keep her warm. The other kayakers headed back to shore.

Becca and Ellie found new strength in their *tired* arms and paddled intently after Tank and Mia. “Tank!” Ellie shouted. “What happened? Is Mia okay?”

“I’m trying to find out. Gotta get her warmed up. She’s pretty shook up.”

“D-didn’t you see ‘em, Tank? Two of ‘em?” Mia spoke through clenched teeth. She was cold and frightened. The ocean breeze played through her wet hair and across her skin, making goose-bumps all over her arms and legs.

“What’d I miss?”

“Fins, Tank! Two fins sticking out of the water. All I could think was ‘shark’. No way I wanted to run into a shark so I stopped paddling, and you ran over me. *That’s* what happened. I’ve never been so scared in all my life. I thought I was going to die!”

“Well, you’re okay now,” said Tank. “I got you.”

“Thanks, Tanker.” Mia could feel Tank’s arms holding her and she was positive that was his heart beating against her back. *Calm down, Mia. Relax. Tank’s got you. Tank’s got me?* Suddenly, Mia bolted upright and pointed. “Over there, Tank! Look!”

Chapter 48
Turn About

Everyone looked in the direction Mia was pointing. Two, no three fins skimmed along the surface of the water not more than 30 yards from the paddlers. Jason held his paddle straight up in the air and stopped the group. Three sleek, gray dolphins rocketed out of the water, did a pirouette, and landed on the surface, creating an enormous splash.

"Wow! There's your 'sharks', Mia," said Tank. "I get how you'd be scared. Geez, I'd prob'ly pass out if I saw a fin in front of me."

Mia leaned back, letting her body relax into Tank again. "They moved so fast. All I could think was shark."

Tank talked over the top of Mia's head and watched the dolphins leap and splash several times before they headed back to open water. "Pretty brave if you ask me," he said. "You didn't even cry."

"No. What *you* did was pretty brave. I could have drowned, Tank. You saved my life."

"I'd do it again, Mia. You're one of my best friends ya know. You're pretty awesome."

This is weird. Tank's never cared about me. What gives?

Jason spun around and paddled back to the two kayaks in tow. "There you go, Mia. Dolphins. They really like to play. You were probably moving so fast they decided to race you, but I've never seen them come into the bay before. Some people think they're good luck."

"But . . . the fins. I . . ." Mia thought about the encounter and remembered seeing them on the way to the island, leaping and playing in the wake of the large fast-moving boat. *But a kayak?*

"Almost all sharks'dorsal fins are triangular in shape," said Jason. Dolphin fins are slightly curved. Bet you'll be able to tell the difference if you go surfing or kayaking again. Let's get you two to shore so the nurse can have a look at you. The rest of us will be back at camp soon."

Being rescued? That's got to be the best good luck ever! I owe Tank big time.

Chapter 49
True Colors

When Tank and Mia got to the beach, Cathy walked the two campers to the infirmary. Mia held onto Cathy and Tank. She limped now and then. "You two doing okay?" she asked.

"I'm okay," said Mia, "just sore from wrestling with that line and seaweed. I got a pretty good bump on my leg. Don't know if I'll ever get into a kayak again. That was ma-jor-lee scary."

"If I know you, Mia," said Tank, "you'll be back at it—sail-boarding, surfing or somethin' way off the charts. Give it a day or two is my bet."

"How 'bout you, Tank?" Cathy was mentally taking notes for the accident report she'd have to write.

"I'm good," was all he offered. "I can take a lot."

Got that right. Mia thought.

Cathy deposited the towel-wrapped campers at the door of the medical lodge and called for the nurse. "She'll be here in minute, guys. Just sit down and wait for her." Cathy left for the camp office, glancing back a couple of times to make sure that Tank and Mia were still seated.

"Tank?" asked Mia. "Back on the kayak, you said you didn't want anything to happen to me. I was like, um . . . your best friend."

"Yeah. Not countin' the guys." He stared at a lizard, sunning itself on the wooden porch. When he wiggled his toes, the lizard scooted into a crack.

"So what'd you mean, I'm pretty awesome?" Mia pulled her towel tighter around her shoulders and tried not to be too obvious in her curiosity. She looked up at Tank's curly red hair, drying in salt-water ringlets. A new respect for the red-haired kid she'd known since Kindergarten was developing.

"Well, you *are*, Mia. No girl beats me at most everythin'. Yer nice. Not mean to me like some *other* people I know. Yer different."

"Thanks. Thought all you cared about was sports, and Twinkies, and Ellie."

"Ah, she's okay. She gets awful uppity sometimes. But, hey. I was plenty scared too, ya know. What if I couldn't of untangled that rope 'n seaweed? You'd a drowned and it'd all be on me."

"Don't go there," said Mia. "You freed me. That's what matters. Thanks for being my friend." *What kind of stupid remark was that, Mia? Shut up.*

"Tank looked at the welt on Mia's leg. Does it hurt?"

"A little. Think I might have kicked the kayak, too. Bet the nurse will just say 'ice it'. That's what they always say when they don't know what else to do." *He actually noticed.*

"You're tough, you know it? Most girls would be crying. That's what I like about you."

There it is again. He likes me? "I'm not near as tough as you when you got hit by that car, Tank."

"Yeah? Well I try not to think about that."

The door opened and Nurse Simpson stepped onto the porch. "Come in, kids. Let's have a look at you."

Tank held the door and helped Mia to a chair inside. The nurse examined Mia's leg and as predicted, offered ice to take down the swelling. "I think you'll be fine, dear," she said. "Just be careful, and stay off your feet for awhile. No more sports 'til you get home. You should probably have your doctor take a look at it, too."

"Darn." Mia looked at Tank. "Our last night here. I was looking to beat you guys at volleyball again."

"And you, young man," Nurse Simpson continued, "incredible rescue. I heard what you did. You should be mighty proud."

Tank blushed. Mia noticed. *Humble, too.*

"Thanks," was all he said, lowering his head.

"Come on, Mia. Put your arm around my neck. I'll help you back to the mess hall. Everybody's gonna want ta see if yer all in one piece."

No argument from me! thought Mia. *What's my dumb heart doing?*

Chapter 50
Packing Up

The following morning Lemon Grove students were breaking camp. Sleeping bags were carelessly rolled, and duffle-bags stuffed. Room 10 was heading home. But something different was happening in the girls' tent.

"What's with you, Mia?" asked Becca. "What did you do to your hair? Did you borrow my lip gloss? I never saw that blouse before either."

"Just trying something. Mom keeps slippin' girly stuff into my bag everywhere I go. Guess she hopes I'll give up the 'tom-boy' life and start being a girl some day."

"Have anything to do with Tank?" Becca was teasing and trying to pry some answers from Mia.

"Not really. Well, maybe. He says he likes me, because I'm tough. I'm not sure what to think. Maybe I just like him because he rescued me. I don't know. Think Ellie will get mad if I like him? If Tank likes me?"

"Remember what I said a thousand years ago? Ellie likes ev-er-ee-bud-ee at some time or another," said Becca. "Don't worry about it. She hasn't said much of anything about Tank lately."

"It's weird. I *might* kind of like Tank. Whatever. You ready for breakfast?"

"Famished," said Becca. "And here comes the queen." She parted the tent flaps for Ellie.

"I'm dying to get home, and get into some decent clothes." Ellie, the high-fashion dresser, for once had to succumb to wearing something twice. "Do I look stupid?"

"Ellie, dah-ling, you look puh-fect," said Becca. "We've been camping for heaven's sake. Aren't you hungry?"

"Not . . . hey, Mia!" Ellie did a double-take. "What happened to you? Trying to impress someone? Like Tank maybe? Just because he got you out of that kayak, doesn't mean you can grab him away from me!"

Mia expected *some* kind of reaction from Ellie, but not the outburst she heard.

"What do mean, away from you? Maybe you think he's cool, but you've barely talked to him this whole trip. Now you're mad at me because I *might* like him?"

"Some friend you are. I don't want to talk about it," said Ellie, and she stormed off to the cafeteria alone.

"Told you she'd be mad," said Mia.

"Don't mind her. She'll get over it," said Becca. "Sometimes she thinks she can control everyone, and it's the first time you've ever liked the same person she likes, or thinks she likes."

"So, she's not my friend anymore, right?"

"Not a chance. You know Ellie. She'll pout for awhile. Besides, who knows what Tank thinks? You and him are always competing and doing stuff together. Maybe he likes you for that. And Ellie's been . . . well, kind of snotty to him. She likes him, she doesn't like him. Know what I mean?"

"Well, her attitude stinks, and I bet she'll stay mad at me forever." Mia's feelings were hurt.

"Don't take it too personal, Mia. Ellie's just being Ellie."

As expected, the four boys were already seated in the cafeteria and were working on second helpings of breakfast.

"Great trip, right?" said Spencer. *Except for the dirty teddy-bear trick. I'll never live that down. Stupid girls.*

"Yeah. Wish we could stay longer," said Zach. "Maybe we can come back sometime." He helped himself to a fourth piece of bacon and poured another glass of juice.

"You're quiet, Tank. Too busy eatin' or is something on your mind? Like Mia maybe?" Alex stirred a piece of toast in the puddle of syrup on his plate and watched for Tank's reaction.

"Leave it, Alex. So what if I do like her? Got a problem with that? She ain't your girl."

"Hey, Man!" He dropped his fork and held up his hands. "No need to get so touchy, Tank. Just kidding. What about Ellie?" Alex backed off once he mentioned her name.

"What *about* Ellie?" Tank answered with resolve. "She's okay, but she's too fancy or somethin'. Mia's more fun. Anyway, it ain't none o' your business, so stay out of it."

When Ellie walked into the cafeteria, she spotted the boys and immediately turned toward the breakfast buffet, her back to them. She sat by herself and picked at the food on her plate.

"What's with her?" asked Spencer. "I've seen that look before and it's never been good. Becca and Mia aren't with her either."

"That's what I mean," said Tank. "Go figure. Somethin's got her all mean again."

Mia limped into the cafeteria with Becca. Tank smiled, and turned crimson when Mia waved at him.

"You got it bad, dude," said Spencer. "Who'd a thought? Mia and Tank."

"Shut up, Spence."

"Cool it, man," said Zach. "You know we're just givin' you a bad time. Besides there's the old "Becca plus Spencer" story and "Alex plus Ellie" who likes nobody and everybody all the time. I wouldn't want her for a girlfriend *any* time."

"Look. They're just friends who happen to be girls and they're stupid sometimes," said Spencer. "That's a fact."

"Ellie's still sittin' by herself. Bet they're in some kind of fight." Zach smiled. "Over you Tank."

"Geez, I said just drop it!"

After breakfast, Cathy and Jason rounded up the group for the hike out of camp. Grampa Potter and Mia rode in the truck with all the camping gear and the box of sack lunches the cook had made for the returning trip home.

The boat ride back to Newly Harbor was much quieter. Ellie was still in a bad mood. She kept to herself, wrote in her diary, and gave everyone the silent treatment. Once, Tank checked on Mia and then returned to play cards with the boys. Mia and Becca sat together and chatted.

"How long is she gonna stay mad?" asked Mia.

"Until she decides she's not mad anymore," said Becca. "Ellie'll think about it and when *she's* good and ready, it'll be over. I think she'll get tired of having no one to talk to, so she'll make up some lame excuse. She'll probably say she likes somebody else, and that you can have Tank."

"I can *have* Tank? Like he's some kind of gift? This is so stupid, and dumb, and weird." Mia was disillusioned by Ellie's anger. "I can't deal with this. Want to play cards?" she asked.

"Sure," said Becca. "Old Maid?"

"Thanks a lot, Becca. Not funny!"

When the boat arrived at Newly Harbor, the school bus was waiting in the parking lot, and Rosa was standing next to it. "Welcome back everybody," she sang out to the campers. "Looks like you all had a great time! What happened to you, Mia? Why the limp?"

"No biggy, Rosa. I'll tell you when we're on the bus."

Once everyone got settled, the bus merged with traffic and headed home. Chaperones slept, kids listened to their radios, played checkers on magnetic boards, or read. Mia sat in the front of the bus where she could stretch out her leg. She explained the kayaking story to Rosa. Becca sat across the isle. Ellie went toward the back of the bus and sat alone, writing in her diary. She stretched herself across the whole seat so no one could sit next to her and glared at anyone who tried.

Two hours later, Rosa pulled the bus into the parking lot at Lemon Grove School and turned off the engine. Anxious parents peered into the bus windows searching for the child they had entrusted to Mrs. Gunderson and the chaperones. Once united with their parents, students talked non stop about their adventure.

"See you Monday or sooner!" Mia hollered after Becca and Ellie. "Take it easy guys." She waved to the boys and got into her father's car. Everyone waved back.

Ellie didn't.

Chapter 51
Home Again

The weekend after camp dragged on and by Sunday, Ellie was bored. She had spoken to no one, and no one had called her. She read and re-read the pages in her diary, ripped out a page or two where she had written less than kind things, and decided that something had to change. She went so far as to scribble out the initials she'd written on the first page of the diary. *Mia was right. I barely talked to Tank at camp. BUT, that doesn't mean I have to apologize and that's that!*

She jumped when the phone rang. *If it's Mia, I'm hanging up. I do NOT want to talk to her.*

"Hel-lo?" Ellie answered hesitantly.

"Hi, um, Ellie?"

"Who's this?"

"Alex."

"Alex, who?" She pretended not to know.

"It's ME. Alex. Sheesh, Ellie, how many Alex's do you know?"

"I get it. You guys drew straws, and you got the short one," she said sarcastically.

"Whatever." Alex wasn't put off. *"You haven't exactly been talking to us lately."*

"So?"

"So I wanted to call you. No straws or nothin'. We're, I mean all of us; me, the guys, Becca and Mia, we're going down to Shadow Falls this afternoon for a swim. You don't have to come, but we're all going, and if you want to come, that's where we'll be. I said I'd call you. So I did."

"I'll think about it. But don't count on it," said Ellie. "Thanks anyway." She hung up the phone. *Hmmm. Alex did this on his own? Wonder if Becca knows anything?*

She picked up the phone and dialed. "Hey, Becca." She said it firmly. "Alex just called me. Says you're all going to Shadow Falls. For real? Or is this some kind of a joke everybody's playing on me? Like you're standing me up or something. And, how come *you* didn't call me?"

"Come on, Ellie. No joke. We just want to get together and celebrate the end of the school year. Kind of a party. No big deal. I was going to call you, but Alex beat me to it. Anyway, that's what we're doing. Come if you want."

"What about Mia?" asked Ellie. "I suppose she's coming? Limping along in some new outfit to impress Tank?"

"How should I know, Ellie? Mia wears what she wears. Besides it's not a fashion show. We're swimming. Whatever you've got going on is between you and Mia. Your problem. Not mine. Get over it. We'll be at the river. Maybe Alex is trying to get your attention. Did you ever think of that? 'Bye, Ellie."

Becca hung up hard and stared at the phone. *You can be so stubborn and stupid sometimes, Ellie Covington!*

The rest of the group wasn't about to let Ellie spoil the day with her moody madness. Spencer and Tank called everyone for the afternoon get together. Alex volunteered to call Ellie.

By two o'clock, Spencer, Alex, and Becca were waiting at Shadow Falls. Grampa Potter showed up in his old truck with Tank and Mia. "You kids be careful!" he hollered after them. "See you later. Have fun!" Tank hovered over Mia, making sure she didn't trip walking to the meeting place. Becca met them halfway and took Mia's arm.

"Your leg is looking better, Mia," said Becca.

"It feels a lot better. Just a lovely shade of yellow now. Dr. Beegle just told me to take it slow. But I'm good."

"Here comes Zach," said Alex, "carrying a bag of something. Ever see a smile that big? Hey, Zach-man! What's up?"

Zach raced to the picnic spot. "I just found out my dad's coming home from the army! He'll be here in time for our last day of school. Mom baked cookies for us. She's practically off the wall happy."

"Wow," said Tank. "That's really cool."

"Yeah, Man," said Spencer. "Bet you and your dad'll have some great talks."

Everyone celebrated Zach's news, and Mia and Becca gave him a big hug.

"So, have a cookie," he said. "Ellie coming?"

"Who knows," said Alex. "I told her we'd be here. If she doesn't show, she's the loser."

No sooner spoken than Ellie's dad drove up and she got out of the van. Ellie held an envelope in one hand and a picnic bag in the other. She motioned and walked up to Mia. "Here," she said, handing Mia the envelope. "I'm sorry, Mia. I guess I've been a real dope. I'd die if you weren't my friend." She reached out for a hug which Mia returned.

Told you so, thought Becca. *She can't function without us!*

"Thanks, Ellie. I'll live. I was hopin' you wouldn't stay mad. So what's in the bag?"

"Well, we can't party without food, so I made a bunch of sandwiches for us, and I brought Tank some Twinkies just for fun and for my personal apology. Sorry Tank."

"Geez, thanks, Ellie. You're all right," said Tank. "I haven't had these for a long time. Been at least a week." He laughed.

The long-time friends ate and reminisced—about camp, the school year, and what would change for all of them next year when they entered middle school. Still, it turned out to be a great weekend after all, and an end-of-the-year celebration to remember.

Tank sat down on his towel, leaned against the tall Sycamore tree and stared at the sky. "Too bad we can't just freeze today forever. Don't this beat all? I mean school's almost out, I got me a really nice grampa, maybe a girlfriend?" He looked at Mia and smiled. "And, I can't believe I, um . . . we actually survived 5th grade. But, best of all, I finally got me some kind o' life!"

Printed in the USA
CPSIA information can be obtained
at www.ICGtesting.com
LVHW032010010823
753870LV00008B/429